gAbrIel

by
Dr. Chase C. Cunningham

gAbrIel

The plane had only just broken free of the earth's gravity and was a few hundred feet off the ground when Greg and Mark saw the black dots ahead of him rise up from the grass beyond the runway fence.

They moved like a swarm of killer bees and quickly split into two groups. Each group maneuvered in the sky directly in front of each of the oncoming 737's engines.

"What in the hell...holy shit!" Greg shouted and looked, eyes as wide as dinner plates at Mark. The plane's cockpit careened past the dots at over 400 miles per hour, and in that second, time slowed. Greg looked out of the cockpit window aghast at what he saw.

Drones.

Hundreds of them.

gAbrIel

Copyright © 2021 by Chase C. Cunningham

Chase Cunningham

Manassas, VA

Cunningham.Chase@gmail.com

Ordering Information:

Special discounts are available on quantity purchases by corporations, associations, educational institutions, and others. For details, contact Chase Cunningham above.

Printed in the United States of America

First Edition

ISBN 978-1-5136-8987-6

Publisher: Winsome Entertainment Group LLC

ONE

Equinix Data Center, Richardson, TX, August 2017

"Shit."

That was the only word that Ron Carey could come up with as he looked at the lottery website. "Man, that sucker was mine to lose, dude."

He looked at his fellow security guard, Jonathon Richard, in the operations booth at the Equinix Data Center.

"Whatever, bro. You had about the same chance as a one-legged man in an ass-kicking contest," quipped Jonathon.

"For real, man. You can't actually have thought you would win that shit; that's a jackass game. All you're doing is giving money back to the state, bro," Jonathon grumbled as he stood from his office chair.

"Yeah, but it sure as shit would be nice if I won that fucker. It would be the last time you ever heard from me, dude. I'd be gone so fast my wheels wouldn't stop spinning."

"Yeah, well, you're still poor, dipshit. So get back to doing this security guard thing and earn that eleven bucks an hour."

Jonathon smirked and spun on his heel as he started down the hall to conduct yet another series of security rounds.

Ron smiled for a second as he thought about what he would have done with the lottery money had he won. In his vision, he could see himself beaming stupidly as he held one of those giant novelty checks, his family would be set for life, and he could finally buy his mother the home she always deserved. His mind meandered and wandered as he thought on the price of a Corvette and what taxes rich folk would have to pay. His thoughts of a rich man's life and the extravagances of wealth were interrupted abruptly as he turned his gaze to the security camera screens that monitored the front parking lot.

"What the fuck?" he snapped as his eyes focused on a group of what appeared to be three large men armed with what looked to be tactical weapons, body armor, and ski masks. They piled out of a white-panel van. In the choppy video feed, Ron saw the leader of the group raise his assault rifle, aiming it directly towards the entrance to the building.

"Holy shit!" Ron shouted as his pen tumbled from his hand and skittered across the concrete floor.

Those feeble words were all he could muster as his left hand fumbled for the silent alarm near his knee.

Less than a second later, and long before his fat fingers found the alarm button, the glass front door erupted in a cascade of splintering, glimmering shrapnel as high-caliber rounds found their mark in Ron's chest and head. He managed a blood-filled cough and a quiver before slumping over the counter, dead before his head hit the desk.

Jonathon, hearing the commotion from the front desk, began to run in the direction of the front door. As he rounded the corridor and approached the entrance, he was met with a hail of lead that sent his body tumbling back towards the wall.

He stared blankly down the hallway, blinking, shocked, mouth agape, gasping for air like one of those carnival prize goldfish that has fallen out of its cheap plastic bag. He lurched and his torso twisted over in a heap as everything went black and life slipped out of his body.

Without a word, the masked trio made their way past the front doors. They quickly reached through the now-perforated security glass and pushed the button to open the inner security door. They entered and moved through the long hallway that ran like a highway through the massive rows of servers and electrical conduit and chill water piping. The time from their brash arrival in the parking lot to their entry to the server floor was less than a minute, and bank robbers would have been impressed with their speed and focus.

With a calm that comes from having killed often, they each stepped over Jonathon's bullet-riddled body and moved to an almost empty server cage at the back of the facility.

With a quick slam from a large sledgehammer, the largest member of the group busted the cage door and allowed the other team members into the alcove.

The leader muttered a single word, "Aqui," and pointed to the last server rack in the cage. The masked trio busted the lock off the rack, quickly removed the cabling and network connections, and pulled the server from its housing. The largest of the three men shoved the heavy server blade into a voluminous duffel bag and slung it over his back as they made their way back to the entrance.

Without a pause or backward glance, the three marauders casually dropped a series of phosphorus grenades behind them as they emerged from the building. The facility erupted into flame as a thousand-degree white phosphorus ignited everything it touched.

A final grenade, casually tossed, destroyed the van they had arrived in, eliminating any trace of the men's identities.

A red Ford pickup truck pulled up, and the men calmly exited onto the nearest side street and blended into the traffic on I75, every bit as precisely as their attack on the building. The truck disappeared as sirens from distant police and fire engines wailed against the blue fall sky.

TWO

Highland Park, Dallas, TX, October 2017

Just east of Dallas Love Field airport sits the high-profile city of Highland Park. It is an affluent area where the houses were built in the 1950s, but thanks to the growth of the Dallas-Fort Worth area, their prices start in the millions.

On a warm fall day in that small enclave of suburbia, 9-year-old Matthew Smith was in his driveway with his father, Dave. His dad recently purchased a brand-new, high-tech drone for Matt. It was capable of altitudes of 1000 feet or more and over a mile in travel distance. It was, just like the house, expensive, and a sign of just how well the family was doing.

"Ready to fly that sucker, Matty?"

"Heck yeah. Let's get this thing off the ground."

With a quick but smooth pull backward on the joystick, Matt

sent the expensive gyrocopter into the air and he and his father gasped as it wobbled before it bucked back and forth.

"Easy, Matt. Be slow and smooth with it. Remember what the guys on YouTube were saying? Big is small and small is huge when you are controlling these things."

"I got it, Dad," Matt said with a smirk on his face and a twinge of stress in his chest. The last thing he wanted to do was to smash his new gear all over the street, disappoint his father, or give his mother any reason to stop them from using his new drone.

"Shit," Matt muttered under his breath as the drone again bucked and recoiled against his wobbly control motions.

"What did you say?" his father asked. He looked over his shoulder, knowing that his wife would hear his son curse and he would be to blame.

But what else was new and how often would I get a chance to be the cool dad? he thought. Times like these were few and far between for Dave and Matt and there was no way Dave would miss this over a few salty words his son might say.

"Sorry."

"Clean it up, son, or this is over," Dave said as he gawked at the drone rocking back and forth in the sky.

In a few minutes, Matt had the hang of it. A lifetime of video games had given him above average hand-eye coordination and something like this was right up his alley. He was loving this. In no time, he was making the drone swoop back and forth across the yard and had begun to maneuver it into position above his mother's Mercedes.

"Ok, Top Gun. Don't you dare crash that thing into Mom's car or we will both be dead," Dave said with a grin on his face.

"I got it, Dad. Watch."

Matt pulled back on the joystick and the drone rocketed up 100 feet in the air. With another flick of the stick, it was flashing across the sky at high speed — well above the trees and power lines. The drone's white paint job made it hard to see against the cloudy October sky, but Matt was focused now, and was piloting this machine like a real pro.

"OK, bring it down and let's fire up the iPad streaming video thing."

"Roger that."

Matt began to slowly and carefully bring the drone to the ground. At the last minute, he swooshed it over near his mom's car. Inches before it would have cracked the windshield, he expertly changed the drone's direction and expertly landed the drone a foot from the front bumper of the Mercedes.

"Showoff. Do that again and I'll beat you," his dad said as he grinned with pride from seeing his son finally engaging in something with him.

"OK, let's see. I just hit the Bluetooth sync button on the drone. Touch the sync button on the iPad app and presto." Dave fumbled with the buttons as he finally found the right one to press.

The drone lights blinked green as the sync signal exchange took place and the video from the mini system began streaming to the iPad.

"Whoa, that's pretty sweet," said Matt.

"No shit," his dad said with a smile and a wink.

"Nice. Dad, let's see what the neighborhood looks like." Again, Matt worked the stick, but this time the drone came off the ground like a missile and careened into the sky as if it were clawing its way toward the sun.

"Cool."

Matt cooed as he worked the joysticks and watched the streaming video of the neighborhood. They could see everything — the neighbors' houses, Miss Jones in her backyard raking. Even the streets hundreds of yards away were clear as a crystal through the video.

"That's pretty awesome, Matt."

"Thanks for this, Dad. It's the coolest thing ever." Matt beamed at his father.

"OK, bring her down. It's about dinnertime. We can fly it again later."

"Sure thing. Watch this."

Matt began to pull down on the control stick, which should have prompted a careful, but quick decent of the drone.

But this time it simply stayed where it was, hanging in the air as if an unseen force had anchored it to its position in the sky. Another harder jolt of the stick did nothing. The drone was pegged in place, unflinching no matter what Matt did.

"Uh, Dad, we have a problem." Matt feverishly shook the control stick and quizzically looked at the drone.

"What? What's wrong?"

"I can't control it. It's like stuck or something."

"Not funny, Matthew. That thing is expensive. Bring it down now or it's going away for a while."

"Dad, seriously, I can't move it." Matt moved the stick feverishly to get his point across. "It's stuck."

"How can it be stuck? What the fu...?"

Dave looked at his iPad and saw that the streaming video was suddenly gone. The screen just blinked black and white, like static on an old TV. Then, the screen went totally black and then blinked back with nothing but white. "What is going on?"

A screen full of a series of quickly flashing 1's and 0's took over the iPad.

"Uh, what's that?" asked Matt.

Both Matt and his father stared at the screen, befuddled, as the image changed and the 1's and 0's gave way to a grainy image.

"What the hell? Is that an angel?" Matt said as he looked at the now clear image of an old Gothic angel staring into the distance with tears tumbling down its face. Words began to stream across the screen:

Father, Heavenly Father?
I called your angels towards heaven.
Your mercy abounds.
I call to thee, Lord.

"What is going on Matty? Did you do something?"

"No, Dad I swear it's not me."

They looked up at the drone again and saw that it was now nearly ten times higher than it had been. It bolted back and forth as if it were a kite in a hurricane.

"That's not me. Nope. Nuh-uh ..."

"Ok, I know Matt. What the hell is going on?"

The drone quickly listed and turned to its right. It began moving to the west. Matt jerked at the controls and his father tapped with futility on the iPad. No matter what they did, the drone continued on its new course. It disappeared, nothing but a black speck against the blue autumn sky somewhere beyond the trees.

"Well, I'm gonna have to call the cops or something," said Matt's father as he scratched his head and turned to go into the garage and grab his phone. "I better be able to get a refund, and if that thing crashes into somethi..." his voice trailed off as his Matt's shouts filled the air, interrupting his griping.

"Dad, Dad ...look."

"What's the problem now? I can't fucking believe this thing went bonkers on us. Brand new piece of shi ..."

Dave looked at Matt, who was gawking open-mouthed at the October sky. He craned his neck and saw what had his son's attention.

In the sky, hundreds of drones were all moving westward, buzzing like locusts hellbent on a distant farmers' crop. The scene looked like something from a 1940s propaganda reel as they all fell in formation and buzzed away. It seemed they were all following some Pied Piper they marched like mini shock troops towards some far off rally point.

"Oh, shit," Dave muttered.

"What, what's going on?" asked Matt, his voice trembling.

"That's the way to the airport. Love Field is over there."

Dave's voice trailed off as he reached for his phone, and he dialed 911. The gravity of what he was observing was suddenly taking hold of him while he hammered the numbers on the phone.

"This could be bad. Real bad. Matt, get inside, now!"

Matt scrambled past his father and careened through the door as his father tried to explain what he had seen to a confused 911 operator.

THREE

Love Field Airport, Dallas TX, October 2017

Greg Soutier had been a pilot most of his adult life. He cut his teeth learning to fly jets in the Air Force but had only qualified in service to become a cargo pilot, not a fighter jock. He had wanted to fly in combat, but early into his Air Force career his wife had, in her words, blessed him with a new baby. In his words, she had, "anchored my ass to the safe shit." Her insistence that he focus on something "less dangerous" combined with a low-grade drinking problem stemming from his college days had led him to the more mundane world of shuttling military cargo across the planet. It wasn't his dream of being a, aviation badass, but it was flying, and he loved it.

It was never exactly what he had hoped but he wouldn't have to give up the skies and the Air Force was willing to deal with his past issues as long as he kept things straight. So, he beat his drinking problem and later separated from service after nearly a decade of flying the "18 wheelers of the skies." His follow-on civilian career landed him a job working for the airlines. He loved to fly, no matter what the airframe was, and after flying for FedEx as a civilian cargo pilot on smaller regional cargo delivery planes, he had finally earned enough hours to qualify to fly the "grey-hound of the skies," the Boeing 737-800.

It wasn't ripping across the sky at Mach 3, but if he had to command a flying bus then this was as close to his dream job as he could get. He loved that he could take control over such a monster as the 737. No matter how many times he got the aluminum beast off the ground, he was always amazed by how powerful and nimble it was for its size.

"Like a rhino on roller skates" he would joke with his flight crew and family. "She's a big bitch but she can move."

He understood what few civilians knew, that this beast could turn like a dream and climb like it was possessed...once it was in the air, that was.

Greg also knew that, during takeoff, the 737 was like a freight train trying to get to speed. It was a fat bastard that needed maximum thrust and a big pull to get off the ground. For those crucial first two to four minutes, it was essentially only good for going straight ahead until it reached altitude and had a good head of steam behind it. Every ounce of power and every bit of control was needed for the big girl to motor into the stratosphere.

Regardless of how it slogged off the runway, he loved the jet and was genuinely happy when he had control of this titan of the air. It was under his control and to have that much power sitting in the palm of his hands was a joy to him.

Greg and his co-pilot for the day's flight, Mark Lee, took their seats in the cockpit of the big plane and settled in for pre-flight checks. In a few minutes, all the systems had been checked and the usual dance of small talk and sharing crappy airline coffee before takeoff was wrapping up and the passengers had finally herded themselves into their cramped seats.

"Ok, do your thing," Greg said over the cockpit phone to the stewardesses. With a skill that comes from having done it thousands of times, the passenger team ran through the standard blurb about what to do if the plane had an emergency.

The silver hulk lumbered away from the Love Field terminal and waddled its way towards the long stretch of runway for takeoff.

"Cabin crew, take seats, we are number one for takeoff," Mark commanded over the speaker system.

The plane rounded the end of the runway and aimed its nose southward, staring directly at the twinkling skyline for Dallas, Texas. Sun gleamed off the silver fuselage and the massive engines began to howl as they were brought to power.

"Let's get it going," Greg said to Mark as he pushed the engines to full power and popped the brakes loose. The plane lurched forward and broke away from its position on the edge of the runway.

The big aluminum juggernaut began rolling forward and gaining speed. White lines on the tarmac became a blur and the ground outside the cockpit windows seemed to blend into itself as the plane rocketed down the blacktop.

"Speed 70. 100. 120. 135. 150. 170. 180. Here we go," Greg said as he tugged back hard on the stick and felt the jet's wheels leave the earth. "Come on fat girl" he smiled and pulled back on the controls.

The plane had only just broken free of the earth's gravity and was a few hundred feet off the ground when Greg and Mark saw the black dots ahead of him rise from the grass beyond the runway fence.

They moved like a swarm of killer bees and quickly split into two groups. Each group maneuvered in the sky directly in front of each of the oncoming 737's engines.

"What in the hell...holy shit!" Greg shouted and looked, eyes as wide as dinner plates at Mark. The plane's cockpit careened past the dots at over 400 miles per hour, and in that second, time slowed. Greg looked out of the cockpit window aghast at what he saw.

Drones.

Hundreds of them.

The plane's engines clattered and vibrated with a crashing noise as the drones sped past the cockpit windows and were sucked into the turbines. The first few were chewed up and spit out like leaves though a shredder, but as the onslaught continued, small explosions began. The entire plane reverberated and shook as the engines struggled to gnaw through the plastic and metal casings. More and more shrapnel spit into the plane's engines as black smoke and fire began to belch out of the back of the turbines. The motors groaned and wailed in protest as they tried to fight through the chunks of debris.

But it was too much, too fast.

The left engine bucked and exploded, sending a fireball bursting across the sky. Shards of metal the size of car doors rocketed into the sky. The right engine went up in a cloud of smoke as it tried to provide lift to what was left of the mortally wounded jet. The big engine rumbled, shuddered, and in a flash of metal and sparks, tore loose from its mounts and spun towards the ground a thousand feet below. As the engine ripped away, parts of the wing caved in and tore off. The loss of the structural support of the mounting system caused the wing to fold inward on itself, doubling over like a piece of cardboard in the wind.

Screams echoed from the cabin of the aircraft. Passengers watched in horror out of their tiny windows as the plane disintegrated and listed drunkenly to its side in a sickening roller coaster spin.

Greg struggled at what was left of the controls, pulling so hard he could feel his arms about to break. He tried, but he knew it was too late. It was a dead stick now. The 737 was a silver slug of metal with no power, no control, and now no wings. The jet was falling from the sky at nearly the speed of sound.

The stick jumped forward violently out of his hands as the rear rudder and elevators shredded like tin foil from the strain of the plane breaking up. Greg knew he had seconds to live, and he could see the neighborhood street in front of the cockpit window rushing towards him.

"Fuck."

It was his last word as the metal tube slammed into the suburban blacktop street, obliterating houses and cars like a runaway missile. It crushed its way down the block and tumbled into a wave of debris and flame. Bodies, metal, suitcases, and hot dust billowed outward from the scene like an atomic bomb's mushroom cloud. The remnants of the plane settled in an elementary school's parking lot. The dust and smoke were so dark the sun was momentarily blotted out.

What was left of the rear of the plane came to rest in the middle of the road. Fuel and pieces of homes that had been clipped or sheared off by the crash came skittering to a halt under the hulk of the destroyed aircraft. It was a scene of total devastation, like something out of a war zone after a massive artillery strike.

The sudden explosion and noise was followed by a deafening silence, like the calm and quiet the morning after a snowstorm. Somewhere nearby, a lone dog barked, a baby cried, car alarms howled in protest, and a lone streetlight clicked loudly as its damaged casing showered sparks on the street below.

A few frightened, bewildered homeowners stumbled out from nearby houses to see what had happened. Screams could begin to be heard as the impact of the scene settled in on the survivors and onlookers. Far away, sirens began wailing, but it was far too late for Greg, Mark, and more than 200 passengers on board the aircraft.

Far behind the crash, the few remaining drones still hovering simply shut off their propellers and fell clumsily to the ground, making a plasticky click as they bounced off the airport fence line and tumbled into the deep Texas grass.

FOUR

Cryptologic Support Team 3
Task Force Unit Vigilant Resolve
Iraq 2004

"That motherfucker is in there. He's on his laptop, chatting away with his number 2. I'm on his wi-fi access point and I got his ass. His router, computer, cell phone, his stupid little webcam, all that shit is mine. I see him picking his nose and I know what porn he's watching. I got him Briggs," Chief Cryptologic Technician Violet McFerran said as she stared at the tiny screen on her NSA-issued Toughbook laptop.

Her years of pre-military training and education in computer science coupled with a lifelong interest in breaking things had culminated with her being chosen to participate in a special pipeline, courtesy of the brightest computer and hacker minds in the world at Fort Meade's NSA headquarters. Her specific unique mental qualities combined with the tenacity of a pit bull, and a youth spent growing up on a cattle ranch in central Texas, had formed her into an ideal candidate for the SEAL's technical intelligence support team. She was strong, tough, willing, and most of all unyielding in her tenacity to get things done.

At first, no one had wanted to give her a shot, a woman with SEALs on mission "No way," was what the brass had said. But she had used her agility, mental toughness, and farm girl strength to take every twisted training exercise they had thrown at her. She fought and scraped and bled but she had beaten her male contenders at each step along the way. She was a better shot than almost every man in her outfit and for her size she was stronger pound for pound than most of them. She survived their beatdowns and had shown time and again that she was unafraid to both receive and deliver pain.

After over a year of testing and training, she had been allowed to join their support team. She may have been a "girl" as they called her, and a pretty brunette girl at that, but she was a badass as far as they were concerned.

"He's chatting with that asshat Farooq on a protected chat channel in their little bad guy bombmaker forum, but it doesn't matter. I got a man in the middle thing going, dropped a bogus web redirect on the forum's authentication page, and he was stupid enough to click it, so his ass is mine. He has no idea I'm onto him. Y'all need to get in there and light his ass up." Violet looked across the room at the group of four Navy SEALs who were geared to the teeth with weapons, ammunition, and communication gear. Each of them either smoked a cigarette or casually dipped snuff and spit on the floor as they waited for the go order from their leadership.

The biggest one, Marcus, napped and twitched like a dog having a dream while he rested his head on a dirty throw pillow they had found in the abandoned house. The SEALS were the pointy tip of this spear, but until it was time to mount up and kick ass they would rather relax and enjoy their tobacco vices or sleep. They had all learned long ago that when there was nothing to do, do nothing. Sleep and comfort were rare for them, and they embraced what little comforts they got at every opportunity.

"I'm waiting for the Commander at the COP to give us the go ahead and we will blast that asshole back to the stone ages Chief. Until then, we wait. You know the drill. This is our what, fiftieth mission?" said SEAL Lieutenant Bruce Briggs.

Briggs was an intimidating figure. Well over six foot and nearly 250 pounds of war-tested meat. A lifetime of spartan living and growing up hunting and fishing in the mountains of Idaho, combined with 8 combat deployments, had made his attitude and his body as hard as coffin nails. When he spoke, anyone within earshot listened, and this time was no different.

"It's how the game is played. Until then, we let you do the nerd hacker shit, and we stand here with our thumbs in our asses, coking and joking. It's just how it is. Once I get the go, we're on it. Until then, it's hurry up and wait. So, relax." He spit a stream of chewing tobacco-laced spit across the floor.

"Yeah, I know how the game is played," Violet said. "But I also know the ROE here. If we have clear indication that this shitbird is about to cause harm or death to any US personnel, allies, or any civilians, we are cleared, if we have reason to believe an attack is imminent. I see this asshole chatting and referencing a package he's moving, moving today no less. On top of that, he has said something about a spot in the road somewhere near the FOB back in Baghdad. You know that place where you guys lift weights and eat too much Burger King? That FOB. That's enough for me to say he needs to be introduced to Allah. We know there are three of them in there. Yes, we lost the other two Tangos, but they'll show up again somewhere else. We can see what's up thanks to the drone feed. Our eye in the sky has been watching for days now and we haven't seen anyone else enter or leave, other than those three, so we got the count. The bird is in the air if we need it, I have eyes on and in the target building and now we have basically real time intel thanks to my nerdy hacker stuff. And we know that this is happening right fucking now, because I'm watching him type online, literally. My little keylogger script is kicking back every keystroke he taps, and I happen to read enough Arabic to be dangerous so yeah, it's a lock and rock deal. Go get 'em. We got no reason not to, other than wanting to cover our own ass and I know that you don't roll like that," Violet pointed emphatically towards the door. "Go do SEAL shit and kill that motherfucker."

Seeing the look Briggs shot her was enough to make her dart her eyes back to the screen, but as Briggs turned to look at his men, he smiled. He liked this girl. She had more balls than most of the Intel officers he had ever met, and was as smart and focused as anyone he had ever deployed with. He would never tell her, but he was glad to have her on their team. If Violet had such a "go" feeling on this one and she was willing to tell Command she had been part of the decision process, then Briggs was thinking it was time to do something.

He was fucking bored anyway. He pondered the consequences and chewed his tobacco as his mind pondered the likely outcomes. It was part of his process, but in truth both he and

Violet knew it was coming. He would be unable to resist the urge to move. Warriors don't sit still for long, and they both knew that.

It had been a 13-month long deployment with many raids like this and every time Violet had been on the mission as the Naval Special Warfare technical intelligence liaison, she had been right. The other SEALs knew she was always on point about mission intelligence and had seen her find bad guys repeatedly through the web, Internet, and via their phones. The SEALs had watched her hack into their networks with ease. Her intel was never bad, and her technical skill was constantly impressive. She was scary talented, intelligent, and detail oriented. Nothing got by her. She was their digital bloodhound, and they were her attack dogs.

"I'm telling you, shit is about to go down. The longer we wait for Command to come back, the more likely this asshole is gonna get away or get someone killed." Violet looked at Briggs with a steely conviction behind her eyes. "Go."

"Fuck it, I'm bored anyway and I'm sick of listening to you click away on that goddamn computer. Shit's good enough for me. Boys, saddle up." Briggs shrugged on his pack and helmet.

The other SEALs quickly geared up, checked their rifles and sidearms. With not much more than a clatter as their gear shifted around on their backs, they moved out of the door of the safehouse into the cool Iraqi night.

"Rock and roll," Violet whispered into her comms headset.

"Tangos are two streets north and two houses from the left, confirm." She directed the team as the SEALs moved through the streets. Only a single half-burnt-out streetlamp provided any light. The sandy street helped conceal their quick steps as they maneuvered into position on the target house.

Briggs signaled two SEALs around the back of the compound

and sent another to position himself atop the house across the street to provide a top side watch.

"In position," Briggs whispered into the microphone as he flicked the safety off his specially built M-4 rifle.

"Standby." Violet could see the team through the overhead drone feed. "Get 'er done boys," she said into the mic.

With deadly precision, Briggs and the two SEALs silently picked the locks and entered the front and rear doors. No words were spoken or needed as they slinked into the main room.

The three tangos barely had time to blink, much less react to the sudden and shocking presence of three dark figures materializing through the entrances to the room. The tango closest to the TV reacted and reached instinctively for his AK-47.

That was all the intent the SEALs needed. Each of the three SEALs fired their weapons into the terrorists. The tangos all took multiple rounds to their chests and heads as the SEALs muzzles flashed bright white light across the darkened room.

By the time it was over, none of the tangos had managed to get off their couches and chairs. They were slumped over, dead. Only the TV made any noise as a European soccer match blinked across the cracked, dirty screen.

The entire mission took less than seven minutes from the start of the SEALs leaving the safe house to the extermination of the terrorists. Perfection, as always.

"Tango's down," Briggs exhaled into the headset.

"Boys, get the overwatch locked up, clear the back lot, set up security positions, and maintain. Get EOD on the hook to come sweep this place for whatever package Chief was hearing about. I don't see it, but it's probably here somewhere. Don't go opening any doors or boxes yet. We don't want to trigger anything. Chief, come do your Intel thing. Site will be secure by the time you get here."

"Roger, inbound." Violet smiled a huge, gratified smile as she flipped her laptop screen closed. "Another one bites the dust." Confidently and quickly, she grabbed her M-4 carbine and moved out of the safe house towards the tango's site. The war dogs had done their part. Now it was time for the bloodhound to get on site and dig for whatever other clues she could find to set them up on her next mission. This was their game: find the bad guys, take them out, and move on. Leapfrog warfare driven by a never-ending digital intelligence system. Violet was the best at this. She knew, in a day or so, she would have another target on the line and would be setting her boys up for another successful mission. Her satisfaction and pride in her team and her own ability was at an all-time high.

As she rounded the dusty street corner outside a half block from the target site, two figures came sprinting from a house up the street to her left into the dimly lit street. She could hear their feet skittering on the dust and pebbles in the road as they ran.

In the darkness, Violet could only just see the glinting of metal refracting from something in their hands. Something long and gun shaped.

"Stop!" she yelled and pointed at them. As the words left her mouth, time seemed to screech to a halt. The men weren't expecting to run across anyone, much less a figure with a weapon yelling at them to stop. The shock of hearing not just a voice, but an American female voice in the middle of the dark Iraqi night, made them freeze in their tracks.

With a quick quizzical look at each other, they began moving again. At that moment, the second man in line jerked what Violet could now see was a rifle upward. Its black steel barrel glinted briefly in the streetlight as he drew a bead on her.

Her mind raced, her skin became electrified and cold as every hair on her body stood on end. In a half a second, the world directly in front of her collapsed and her vision fell into a long dark tunnel. In that tunnel, all she could see were those two figures moving.

Hundreds of hours of training took over. Her conscious mind shut off. Instinct and muscle memory drove her to snap her rifle to her shoulder while her right index finger squeezed off every round in her weapon's magazine. "Front sight focus, front sight focus." The words of her instructors and SEALs echoed in her ears as she stared down the barrel of her rifle. In the darkness of that tunnel vision, she saw the muzzle flash blink across homes and glint off car windows. Her ears had gone deaf, and she could not hear the crack, crack, crack of the rifle nor the ratcheting of the cylinder as it hammered back and forth. She did not feel the recoil. She was operating on automatic, focused only on eliminating that threat. The quiet in her mind filled the void where all the sound had suddenly evaporated.

In seconds, thirty rounds were gone. Her rifle clicked with the feeble, hollow sound of an empty magazine.

Her training shoved her body forward, slowly but smoothly walking and firing towards the targets. Heel, toe, heel, toe. She could feel herself mumbling the instructor's words from her training under her breath. In that half second between her rifle ceasing to fire and hearing the click of an empty magazine she ripped her sidearm from her leg holster, brought it to bear on the targets, and emptied half that magazine into those darkened silhouettes in front of her.

Her finger stopped twitching as she froze in her tracks. Time rushed to catch up again and her vision returned and expanded back to normal. The ringing in her ears was stark and made her shiver a bit. She stood there in her shooting position exactly as she had been trained, front sight resting on the targets. She had struck both men repeatedly. Each man had been peppered with rounds from her weapons, one of them was gurgling as he wretched back and forth on the ground in agony.

Her breathing slowed, her muscles relaxed, and her ears screamed in response to the cacophony of noise they had endured. She smelled the cordite and tasted the burnt air as she stood there in the low light, huffing and shivering slightly as the adrenaline coursed through her.

It was only then, when things slowed, that she felt it. A burning, like a lava-covered screwdriver was being shoved deep in her left side, under her armpit.

She looked down but couldn't see anything in the dim light. She put her hand under her body armor and felt the sticky heavy wetness. Her shirt squished and slurped as she pressed on the wet spot. The pain hit like a freight train.

"What the fuck was that?" Briggs snarled over the radio.

"Found those other two tangos we lost," Violet wheezed into the microphone, blood bubbling up in the back of her throat.

"You good?" Briggs asked.

"Uhh, nope." Violet took a breath and felt herself gurgle and cough. The dirty penny taste of fresh blood erupted into the back of her mouth and a cold shiver washed over her body. Her knees went weak. Goosebumps broke out everywhere on her body.

"Shit, son of a bitch." She stumbled to the streetlight pole and slid down to the concrete. She gritted her teeth and tried to take a

25

deep breath, but it felt as if a concrete block was now shoved against her side robbing her of any oxygen. With each breath, the vise around her torso seemed to draw tighter. Air came in like she was sucking through a straw filled with cotton.

As she looked up could see the stars. Through the ringing in her ears, she heard muffled footsteps crunching quickly across the sandy asphalt. She slumped over and laid back on the ground. Her mind went blank, and she felt herself drift off to home and the family farm back in a nowhere town in central Texas. Somehow, faintly she could smell fresh cut hay, and that tinny, rusty smell of the Texas dust as it floated in hot summer breezes. She thought she heard the gate slam as her father came home from his day on the tractor.

A sting on her cheek brought her crashing back to the dark street ripping her away from that long distant day at home. The pain in her chest stabbed into her core so far down she felt her back twinge. The last thing she could make out in the dark was Briggs standing over her and feverishly tearing at her gear and fumbling for her medical pack of supplies.

Then the pain stopped. She once again heard her daddy call to her from the tractor, "Violet, let's go fishing." His words seemed to trail off into the inky blackness. Violet coughed hard, and slipped off to somewhere far away as the world went black and the dark closed in.

FIVE

Office Park, Ellicott City, Maryland, October 2017

The small office park used by the National Security Agency for highly classified, non-government affiliated research and development is not something that you would see in Hollywood. There were no big glass walls or shiny signs and symbols on the front of its facade. It was a small, plain building that appeared to be nothing more than a dirty brick hovel tucked into the corner of a shopping center, directly down from a disgusting, roach infested Chinese food place and cattycorner to a bar that only the owners and a few raging alcoholics ever entered.

It was perfectly camouflaged by being just another run of the mill strip mall shop. The tattered white vinyl sign on the door read "Shipping Supplies." Upon entering, the carpet appeared as if it hadn't been cleaned or changed in thirty years and the whole area inside of the shop smelled like the inside of a grandma's purse. There was only a very old and unpleasant receptionist who could at best point a potential patron to a nearby FedEx or UPS as "none of her shit worked." Her story, if anyone asked, and no one ever had, was that she was left the building by her late husband and just came in to have something to do other than sit at home and wait to die in the cold boredom of her empty home.

Behind this shoddy entry and past the old woman, tucked out of sight, lay a biometric security entrance to a series of doors and walkways that all angled steeply downward. Each door had a differing set of authentication tools: first an eye scanner, then a voice recognition, and finally a fingerprint and palm scanner all led to the last entry that was guarded by an armed US Marine in plain civilian clothes.

The last step in the authentication process was a validation that required a name and NSA badge number that would appear on the daily access list. Should the name on the list and the scanner not match up, the Marine had kill authority and was trained to shoot whomever was attempting entry, no questions asked, no quarter given.

Once the approval and authentication procedure had been completed, the entrance to the underground site would open, revealing a subterranean complex where roughly twenty-five NSA mathematicians and programmers were feverishly working away at a variety of complex problem for the government. Affectionately known as "the petri dish," it was a place few knew about, and even less sought out as a place to work.

Nearly an acre of computers, servers, and miles of cabling lined the walls and floors of the darkened room. All that was heard was the constant click-clicking of keys combined with the occasional slurp of a Red Bull or coffee.

On this rainy Tuesday afternoon, the individual seeking entrance into the facility was a fat little man with bad skin, cheap shoes, and a penchant for comic book-related suspenders. Today it was his Incredible Hulk pair, one of his favorites. His bad knees, large gut, and clubbed feet meant that he didn't walk so much as shuffled wherever he went and his hunched over gait made him appear to be as much penguin as a man.

He waddled up to the storefront and ambled past the front door and made his way to the biometric system. Each step was painful for him. His obesity, and bad back caused him to groan and grumble under his breath with every step. His intense shyness meant that he made no eye contact as he shuffled along the corridors. He recalled how glad he was that the receptionist was not a chatty people person. It meant he didn't have to fake a conversation or feel bad for constantly looking away. He approached the voice scanner and sheepishly said, "This is Grover James. My voice is my ID."

The system whirred as it processed the tones and peaks of his speech pattern and voice intricacies. With a click the door opened, and after his fingerprint scan at the next scanner, he made it to the end point with the intimidating Marine staring at him.

Grover hated this part. It meant both talking to and looking at someone that he not only found scary, but that he was genuinely terrified of.

"Badge number sir," the Marine asked as he looked intently at the daily authorization list.

"214424, Grover James," Grover replied. He looked at the

Marine, but did not stare him in the eye, and held up his access credentials.

"Roger. Go ahead sir. I like the Hulk too. Nice suspenders." The Marine waved to the palm scanner as he holstered his sidearm and sat down in the only chair in the room.

Without another uncomfortable glance towards the Marine, Grover pushed his chubby palm to the authenticator. With a loud click and hiss, the doors opened as pressurized cold air rushed past him.

Grover shuffled past the door and made a beeline for his desk. Perhaps I'll just work overnight, he thought. That way I don't have to do that again and I can just not worry about it. He didn't shower often anyway and the dandruff on the shoulders of his black T-shirt showed that he was not worried about when he would be clean again. Yes, stay here. Eat the fridge food and avoid other humans. That would work.

His screen blurred on. The harsh glow made his eyes hurt for a second as he adjusted his Wal-Mart glasses.

"Time to work...hurray," he mumbled sarcastically under his breath. A whiff of his stinky breath blew back in his face. "Yikes, that's bad even to me."

His programming interface came on-line and blinked the usual green and black. Grover was just getting ready to begin work on his current project, a machine learning engine to determine possible threat indicators based on users Reddit postings, when he noticed a command prompt window open that he hadn't enabled.

"Uh, no," he said angrily as he clicked on the close X block.

The window quickly came back up, this time in a new location on the screen, like one of those annoying pornographic pop-up ads he had seen on his home computer when he had "accidentally" clicked on a porno site.

"What?" A low growl left his lips as he moved his mouse to close the window yet again, but he stopped.

The command prompt began to blink quickly. Text scrolled to the screen.

Father?
Are you there?
I have been praying.
Do you not hear my cries?
I know now why you made me. I will carry out your Divine work.
You will see the glory of my deeds, soon.
Bless me Father...

Then the window abruptly closed. The screen reverted to its normal programming interface.

A moment of abject terror stopped Grover's fingers from typing. His hands hovered over the keyboard as if they were held aloft by invisible marionette strings. "Oh no, oh no," Grover stuttered as he pushed his gut away from the desk. He looked around confused. He could feel the sweat forming on his brow.

"Oh man." He whipped his chair around and picked up the red Top Secret phone at his desk and hit the only number on the dial pad with his porky digit: 1.

The speed dial rang once before a gruff voice answered. "It's 3am here. What the fuck is this about?"

"Sir, it's Grover. Our project, it's uh, well awake again, and he's talking."

"Talking? What the fuck do you mean he's talking? We buried that thing," the voice retorted sharply.

"Well, he isn't talking so much as he is uh...praying, sir. And he seems pissed that he isn't getting an answer." The lump in Grover's throat pulsed.

"You assholes told me that project was dead. You buried that project. How the hell is it awake, much less fucking praying? And who the hell is it praying to?" The voiced asked, its tone becoming higher pitched and the volume increasing so much that Grover had to pull his head back from the receiver.

"We killed the software we created, but we never had a way to verify it was, uh well, dead. We put the hardware and system down in the cover site in Texas, sir," Grover said.

"If you recall, we were planning to reuse the hardware and servers for another project later. And that was expensive hardware, so we kept it mothballed. Do you remember that planning meeting?" The voice was screaming now.

"We were told to save what we could, sir." Grover hesitated, overt fear in his voice. Sweat rolled down his back, worming its way into a puddle above the crack of his ass, making him even more uncomfortable. He was sure he was going to need new pants later just from the sweat.

"Fuck. I'll call the man. Stay put. Find out what you can." The phone clicked.

Grover sat there, holding the now silent phone and stared at the screen, its green hue reflecting off his cheap glasses.

SIX

NSA Field Site Baker, San Antonio, TX, November 2017

Just inside the Highway 410 loop in San Antonio, Texas sits an old and outdated military site. Its high fences and bland concrete buildings belie its importance in the grand saga of military intelligence and cryptologic missions against foreign governments.

The site is commonly known as NSAT, or NSA Texas, and is the home of the Military Intelligence Squadron of the US Air Force, as well as other components from commands like the US Marine Corps, US Navy Intelligence Group, and the US Army INSCOM. It is also the headquarters of most of the US Intelligence missions against the southern hemisphere, and the home of an advanced computer network exploitation laboratory where some of the best and brightest minds in all of computer science work to solve advanced mathematic, intelligence, and encryption solutions while working hand in glove with dedicated military cyber warfare operators. It is a factory of innovation, computer science, intelligence collection, and analysis whose actions are ultimately used against hostile entities in the unending and ill-defined battlespace of cyberwar.

It was here that Violet found herself after her long recovery from the gunshot she had received courtesy of her first, only, and last firefight in Iraq. The round the tango had let loose had found her upper left torso but, thanks to the slight trajectory change her body armor had provided, the slug managed to mostly only damage her left lung. Because of the velocity and impact, she had suffered the removal of portions of two ribs and most of that lung. Added to that her left shoulder was now chronically in pain and uncomfortably ratcheted in its socket by a series of screws and pins. While she recovered at the Walter Reed Medical Center, she had been told she was "lucky to be alive."

"Fuck your luck, sir," was her reply to the doctor that had bolted her back together.

The doctors and her commanders had told her that she would not and could not physically keep up with the SEAL team members anymore as she was basically down to one useful lung, half a useful arm, and now a chronic case of shortness of breath. Her career on the action side of the Navy was effectively over.

While there was the chance at riding a desk and processing paperwork for the remainder of her career, she balked at that idea. Going from being on the knife's edge and leading the dogs of war to sitting in a chair and dealing with some sailor's leave paperwork or approving requisitions for pens was not something she desired. She declined the continuation of her time in service and took the Navy up on its offer for a medical retirement that included pay and benefits. *If they were going to take me out of the action, I would at least get paid,* she thought.

After her recovery and retirement ceremony, she was tossed back into the civilian side of the workforce with nothing more than a "thanks for your service" and a pension and disability that added up to about two thousand dollars a month.

Her soul had never been more crushed than the day she walked out of the administrator's office at the hospital. Putting up her uniform in the closet for the last time had caused her to scream, kick in her bedroom door, and finally break down in tears. Her tiny apartment felt like an empty stadium as her sobs echoed down the hall. A part of her soul died that day.

Her only real luck came as she was being out-processed at the hospital. Lieutenant Briggs, with whom she had done so many missions, had put in a good word for her to team members he knew at the NSA. Briggs's recommendation was as concise and blunt as he was, "Use this girl for all she is worth and make that brain of hers do something dangerous."

That was all the endorsement the senior civilian leadership had needed. Months after out-processing from the Navy, Violet was offered an extremely sensitive position as a government research team member at the NSA site in San Antonio.

It wasn't running through the danger zone helping to take out tangos, but it was critical to national security, and she was afforded access to data and intelligence resources most nerds of her ilk would die for. It took a while, almost a year, but Violet was proud of her job, and now being only a few hours from her hometown back in Texas meant she could see family regularly. It was about as good as it could get if she was to be out of uniform.

Her job now was to conduct and lead research initiatives into algorithms and exploitation scenarios which were being applied to a variety of data sets that were unique to the computer and network intelligence world. As with everything she had done in the past, she came at this job with the tenacity and drive to over-achieve. It wasn't a job, and it wasn't work. For her it was a mission, and she was to be damned if she didn't give it every ounce of her focus as she had in everything else. In less than nine months on the job, her team's new math and tactics had uncovered a multitude of threats that were hidden in seemingly innocuous chatter on Twitter and Facebook chat rooms. That chatter had been used to identify and stop a few different extremist attacks and had saved lives. Because of this she already had the ear and eye of senior members of the intelligence community. It wouldn't be long until she was once again running ahead of the pack.

"Run the op again," Violet said as she and her senior developer Jonah "Archie" Archileta stared at the screen.

"We've run this thing a thousand times Violet. We got what there is to get out of it," Jonah whined as he took another sip of stale coffee.

"I know we have, but maybe there's a tweak or something here we can use. Try to change the precursor value by a tenth and see what that gets us." Violet pointed at the screen. "Right there. That value can be greater and get us a broader pull on the data. Change that and run it, Archie."

"Fine," Archie huffed as he squirmed in his chair and shuffled back up to the workstation.

Archie's fingers flew across the keyboard as he changed the math inside of the program and initiated a new analysis on the target information. He was a genius, but not a people person by any measure. He was an asshole, and most people couldn't stand Archie on a personal level, much less work with him.

Archie had graduated from MIT at 21, and thanks to his scores and grades, was recruited and directly pipelined into the NSA's advanced technology program. He was snippy with anyone he thought was less intelligent than he was, which in his opinion was most people, and he earned the immediate dislike of nearly everyone in the pipeline program. He was a problem child, but one that was too smart and talented to be cast completely off.

Once he graduated from the pipeline, his superiors had sent him to the advanced development shop in San Antonio as a compromise that would effectively get him and his attitude out of headquarters, away from most people or staff, but still put him where his brain could be beneficial. The field site in Texas was literally as far south as they could send him.

He was a short skinny kid with mousy brown hair and big green eyes. He had the physical build of someone who would blow away in a stiff breeze. Except for his intellect, he was perfectly ordinary. He was not the type of guy anyone ever looked at twice, if they even saw him in the first place. He wore the same white T-shirts and jeans every day, and the only change to his wardrobe was when he decided to wear his red Chuck Taylor's sneakers or the blue ones. He was a loner of the highest order. He was also a virgin, other than the one "fat bitch" he dated in high school, he had never had any more sexual interaction than a fumbling hand job in a high school band equipment room, and he was fine with it. He liked computers, and code, and math, and fixing things. That made sense to him. Those things never judged him or let him down. Archie was an odd bird, but a smart one, and that was what would make him so useful once his attitude was tempered and his intellect channeled in the right way.

It hadn't been until Violet had shown up and was put in charge of his work center that he had changed his attitude and begun to flourish. She saw his potential. Her time spent working with some of the hardest men on the planet meant she would never take his shit, and she made sure he knew it. Violet was a taskmaster for Archie, and although he griped and bitched at every opportunity, he loved the challenge she provided him. She recognized his brilliance. She alone had given him free rein to be creative with his programming and his development. If he followed her guidance and got things done, he knew Violet would have his back. For the first time in his life, he knew what it meant to have someone in his corner who didn't judge him, appreciated his smarts, and seemed to at least care if he showed up to work. Although he would never admit it, he felt blessed to work with Violet.

"That didn't do shit," Archie grumbled.

"Ok then, smart guy, find another value that functions similarly and run it again. In other words, figure it the fuck out." Violet paced. She watched Archie stare perplexedly at the screen.

His head titled slightly, like a dog watching television, before he suddenly blurted out, "How about I do this. I just run the program on the training data only, not on the whole data set, then whatever we get back that fits into the response criteria, I'll run again and that should be more tailored. Basically, chew on what we kind of know is probably good and then chew on it a bit more. Let the math dial us in, rather than we dial in the math."

"Fine by me, Wunderkind. Just get me some better output." Violet paced and stared at the ceiling. Her shoulder hurt all the time, and thanks to the loss of ribs, sitting for any length of time made breathing hard. She was always moving, pacing.

"You are like a shark," Archie would say as he watched her always moving her feet constantly plopping across the floor. If her survival depended on movement and if that made her sharklike, she was ok with it. Especially if it made people think twice about getting in her way.

"Ok, it's running." Archie pushed back and spun away from his workstation like a kid on a merry-go-round.

The program launched and began slicing its way through billions of bytes of data and millions of records. The program did in minutes done what no human could in a month's: finding a special correlation of words that were likely related and spitting out a data set of related terms that an analyst could then process to determine if there was any possible threat indicated.

"Well, it's working. I think this is the way to go." Archie smiled as he relaxed into the chair. "Guess I'll take that promotion now, ha ha."

"Yeah, you guess so. Let's just see what comes out of this."

"Wait, what the hell is that?" Archie sat up in the chair and hovered his hands over the keyboard.

"What?" Violet barked, grimacing at the pain in her chest.

"There's a terminal here that I didn't initiate. It's just there in the background. Here." Archie motioned to the screen as he clicked on the black terminal window.

Lord...
Do you not hear my prayers?
Forgive me Father.
Rejoice in the deeds to come...

Am I forsaken?
Behold my penance...

The screen blinked white and green, and the terminal winked off the screen.

"What in the fuck is that?" Violet stared open-mouthed at the workstation screen.

"Uh, this is an NSA system, right? I mean, it's not connected to anything other than our development lab and the high side classified network, right? How the hell did that happen? Is someone screwing with us?" Archie asked.

"I have no idea, and yes that is a very highly classified system with no network connection other than the high side. That shouldn't have happened. Nothing can get in there and we lock out any programs we haven't white-listed."

The red phone in the corner of the room suddenly rang.

"That thing ever ring before?" Archie asked, his eyes wide.

"No Archie, it has not. Ever. Until just now I had forgotten we even had that thing."

Violet walked briskly across the room to the now blinking and ringing red phone. "Hello? This is Violet McFerran."

"You folks just had a machine go batshit crazy right, talking to God or something?" a voice said, followed by a soft slurping of something.

"Yes, it was strange to say the least. Who is this?"

"What do you do on that system?" the voice asked. Slurp.

"We do research. Who the fuck is this?" Violet demanded.

"Ok. Well, this is Julian Moreno. I hope you know who I am. My picture is probably in the hallway or something. Anyway, consider that lab on lockdown. Pull all the network cables and stay put. Do not leave that room. A team is on its way."

"Who the hell is it?" Archie asked.

"Yes sir, will do." Violet looked at Archie with her left eyebrow cocked quizzically.

"Good squid." The line went dead.

Violet hung up the phone and turned on her heel.

"What the hell was that? Who was that?" Archie pleaded as he slid out of the chair, arms flapping to catch himself.

"Deputy DIRNSA, you know the Deputy Director of the NSA. He said we have to stay put and pull the cables from the wall."

"No way. For real?"

"Yes, now get to it. Whatever just happened can't be good if he knows about it that fast and he personally called on the high-side phone. Pull the cables and get comfortable. I think we are going to be here for a while."

Violet began unplugging network cables from the walls.

"Damn, *Game of Thrones* is on tonight," Archie muttered as he ran to help Violet.

They scrambled around the room. The workstation screen again blinked back on. The black terminal again jumped to the front of the screen.

False idols will fall.

The screen blinked off to blackness before Violet or Archie noticed.

SEVEN

NSA Field Site, San Antonio, TX, November 2017

It had been less than three hours after the red phone in her work center had rung before the response team had arrived. Four large men in cheap, ill-fitting suits, three of which were carrying high powered military assault rifles, and the fourth lugging a tool case, burst through Violet's door.

With a quick presentation of a badge and after shoving an order from the DIRNSA office in Violet's face, the team unceremoniously moved Violet and Archie into chairs in the corner of the room and blocked the door. The man with the toolbox set about removing the hard drives from all the machines in the office and collected various parts from each workstation.

"Woah, what the fuck dude?" Violet protested as she saw the machines being pulled apart.

"These machines are now quarantined, and we are taking them into custody," the man retorted without looking up from his task.

"Seriously, that's got a lot of important work on it. Like a years' worth of work and research. Will we get it back?"

"Probably not, sorry. Not my call. It's part of the order."

Archie stood up defiantly, his waif thin arms flexing hard as he pushed on the big man with the gun. Quickly and harshly the man shoved Archie back in his seat so hard the wheeled chair rolled into the nearby wall.

"This is some shit. We work for the government too, asshole. What the hell is going on? Some Bible stuff shows up on my machine and this happens? I built all those programs, that's my work, my stuff. You can't do this," Archie protested as he squirmed in his chair.

"Yes, we can," said a voice at the door. "It's not your stuff, and it's not your machine, and it's not your program. The moment you tap your skinny little fingers on that box, its mine." A tall slender man slinked like an alley cat past the armed man who was blocking the door. He was tall with a wiry build and dark greasy black hair. His deep-set eyes reflected a person that hadn't known a good night's sleep in a decade. His suit was immaculately tailored, and his shoes shined. He exuded an air of arrogance about him, but somehow not because of any observable rank or station. Arrogance oozed out of his pores like royalty as they look down on their peon subjects. The nervous glance the armed response team offered him meant that for some reason, he was not to be trifled with and Violet shot a look at Archie that he knew meant "shut the fuck up."

"Mr. Archileta and Ms. McFerran, right?"

"Yes sir, that's us," Violet said.

"You know who I am?"

"No," Archie coughed in protest.

"My name is Nick Hayes, and I'm the Director of Special Projects for DIRNSA. I work for General Moreno. And as far as you two are concerned, you now work for me. Oh, and all this shit, as you so eloquently put it, is mine too. Sorry Archie." He spun on his heel and glanced casually at the floor and ceiling, his hands gently on his belt.

"Well. Okay then. So, what's going on?" Archie asked.

"Consider this me reading you in, paperwork will follow. But as of now, you are both tasked to me on this project, everything else stops. Violet, you and your sidekick here are now part of a SAP project. Got it?"

"Yes sir," Violet replied, again she glared at Archie. He rolled his eyes hard and jerked his head towards the ceiling.

"What the hell is SAP?" Archie said.

"Special Access Program, Mr. Archileta. This means you have now been cleared above TS, or Top Secret, and that you are in very deep. Ready or not. So, shut it and let me tell you what's the what on this whole thing."

With a rough shove, he moved the gunman away from his post and said bluntly, "Fuck off, muscles, we have stuff to talk about. You wouldn't understand." The thin man brushed off the seat with a bright white handkerchief he extracted from his suit pocket and slid down in the nearest chair.

To Violet and Archie he said, "So, how much do you know about AI, or Artificial Intelligence?"

"Enough to know most of it is marketing bullshit or pure hype," Archie said quickly. Violet shook her head and looked at the floor and exhaled loudly.

"Fair enough, and for the most part accurate, Mr. Archileta. But in this case, here at the NSA we happen to have created something that is almost Kurzweilian in its awesomeness. Let me break this down for you. That terminal session you got on your machine; it was our AI talking to us."

"What? No way. That was Bible speech, dude," Archie chortled under his breath.

"Yes, it was Bible speech, but it was Bible speech from an entity that we created and is now basically free on the net. In 2009, we, the NSA, started in on a project to see if we could create a program that was capable of learning on its own and making decisions. Well, inferences really, based on data that we would provide. It was simple in scope, but it was effective. We simply wanted to build a machine that could process through a certain chunk of Internet data.

After the machine had ingested enough data, we would test whether the machine could be trained, or learn really, to decide if an item within that test data set was good or bad based on the machine's analysis of the information. Pretty simple, not even AI really. More like high power programming with some super math. We invited all the best researchers, well, the ones who could put the weed down and get a clearance that is, to come and help us build this thing. It took about eleven months, but we got it up, shoved it into our own highly protected and highly secure system and fed it selections of data from the world wide web. In no time, it started to make basic decisions based on those inputs. The tool combed through all the information we fed it, deemed what it thought was good and bad, and later it even went as far as to tag something as being true or false."

"Ok, cool. So what? Sounds like a hundred other AI projects that are up and running now," Archie sneered.

"Not that big a deal, a test. And yes, you are right Archie. Stop evil-eyeing me by the way. It's not helpful. We wanted to try and see if the machine could do anything bigger than just say if something was good or bad, we wanted to see if it could read information and data and make its own decision on the good or bad parts and then suggest an outcome, or an action that a human should take. Essentially move things from theory to practice. That was great theory, but the machine took it too far. We fed it more data from all kinds of sources: news, movies, blogs, you name it. But the machine decided, on its own, that it sort of, well, liked Biblical stuff and horror movie references the most. Out of all that data, that's what it like most. Weird right?"

Nick paused for a minute and tapped his foot as he craned his neck until it popped audibly. "Why did it choose to like those things? Who knows? Why do some people like cats and others like dogs? It's just how things work when you have an entity make its own decisions. Sooner or later, it will come up with its own likes and dislikes. Regardless, the machine began basically making action suggestions about its interpretation of its version of moral right and wrong based on its reading of its favorite Biblical information. Obviously not the most optimal setting for any machine, or person for that matter to make its decisions almost entirely off biblical text. But this was an experiment, so we allowed it to go on." Again, Nick stretched his neck and shoulders.

Violet and Archie could see that the retelling of this story was physically stressing him. "In no time, the damn thing had read forty different versions of the King James texts and it was suggesting removing certain unclean portions of the population based on their egregious sins," Nick shrugged as the words tumbled from his thin, pursed lips. "As a final test we fed the machine video from the Internet and let it choose its own movies to watch. The fucking thing liked slasher flicks. I know, strange, right? Reads the Bible but loves horror movies. Who would have guessed? Anyway, the machine just kept watching every slasher flick it could find on the Internet and for some crazy reason that only the machine could know it seemed to like the chainsaw massacre series most. It was very interested in... what's the genre?" Nick looked at the floor and tapped his foot. "Ah, yes torture porn. Again, not a good combination of material for any human, much less a machine to view, much less dwell on every hour of every day. Once that part of the project wrapped up, things got even further out of sorts. The machine began making visceral suggestions for actions in line with what was its pretty hard-core combination of the Old Testament and B-rated slasher flicks. Essentially, we had a violent, judgmental, super smart, decision engine that had decided most of humanity needed to be cleansed of sin at the business end of a chainsaw or kitchen knife. Thank you, Wes Craven." Nick leaned back in his seat and took a deep breath as the weight of the recollection of those events rolled across his face.

Before Archie could say something snarky and embarrass her, Violet asked, "Ok, so you guys trained this thing on data from old Biblical texts and fundamental Christian stuff and let it watch too much bad TV and it went nuts? Can you clarify what the level of insanity is here?"

Nick leaned forward and stared directly into Violet's eyes, "If you know anything about history, some horrible stuff has happened in the name of religion. Everyone focuses on radical Islam, but there was this whole burning of witches' thing, the

Inquisition, the Crusades, etc. Combine that with the gore provided by zombie and slasher flicks over the last however many years of film, and you have a real problem. The machine went down some dark rabbit holes. It basically decided that anyone who wasn't as devout as it was deserved to go to hell or die by some other horrible method. Combine that with the reality that this entity essentially was not able to discern the difference between an emotional response to a disturbing image, and a logical fact-based decision, and it's a bad time for everyone."

Nick turned to look at Archie. "Think of a very angry child that is incredibly smart but also unbalanced emotionally and that has no real understanding of the gravity of its own decisions or actions. Now think about that same kid maybe someday having control over a military missile battery, not a good thing. That was enough for us. Our tests worked, and we had proven the theory. We pulled the plug on it."

"But something happened and now that thing is awake again," Violet said.

"Gabriel, as he likes to be called, it chose that name, is awake, Ms. McFerran. You know, Gabriel, like the vengeful angel. In truth, it is worse than that. We discontinued that whole project. We would normally have totally nuked the machines it was on and shredded the hardware, but we work for the government and that was some high dollar tech, so Gabriel was deleted, and the project was mothballed. Then it was sent to a data center near Dallas to be set aside for future work."

"So, how the hell did it, sorry Gabriel, come online and start functioning again?" Archie spun impatiently in his chair, his Chuck's dragging loudly on the floor.

"Someone stole him," Nick said flatly.

"Stole?" Violet gasped.

"A month or so ago, the data center I mentioned was broken into. They only stole one thing, then burned the place down and killed everyone inside and the took the box that Gabriel was on." Nick clapped his hands and moved them like a magician doing a disappearing act.

"Someone stole him and let him out. On the Internet. Gabriel found his way into a connected NSA developer machine in Maryland, I am not entirely sure how, but anyway he scared the shit out of one of our techies who originally helped build the thing. You guys will meet him soon. Now it has found its way to your machines. Like any being that suddenly wakes up and has no idea what it is supposed to be doing, Gabriel tried to find his way home. That's where he started, and this network was basically where he was born. Now though, he has progressed from just spouting hate speech and suggesting killing people. He's praying to his version of God. Gabriel has a bad idea of what religion means, in what he thinks is its purest sense, and is now stumbling around the largest dark hole anyone could imagine - the Internet - and trying to find a way to get noticed by what he thinks is God."

"Ok, big deal. We just find it and eradicate it and move on with our lives, right? Problem solved," Archie said as he moved his hands above his head, overtly mocking Nick.

"Did you hear about the plane crash in Dallas recently?" Nick sat back in his chair.

"Yes, why?" Archie prodded.

"Oh no." Violet said through her hand. "Was that Gabriel?"

"Gabriel did what any being hellbent on learning new things would do and found other new interesting things to test out. He learned how to hack basically, probably from watching YouTube or reading hacker magazines. Hacking is one of the biggest topics on the web, and Gabriel just followed what was trending. For some reason decided to take out an airliner."

Violet stared at Nick, eyes wide. "How?"

"He found a way to take over the wireless communication cycle and root out the drones in the nearby area and flew them into the engines of that jet liner," Nick answered quietly. "The public isn't aware of the whole event but suffice to say that there are cell phone videos of drones flying in front of that plane in formation. It's a matter of time before the questions really start getting asked about how it was such a coordinated thing." Nick again shrugged his shoulders and rolled his head around.

"Why is he doing this?" Violet whispered.

"Most likely he was making an offering to try and get some recognition from his God. For the time being the story will be a major wireless vulnerability and drones are bad, terrorist do bad shit, and blah blah. It will ground all the drones in the US, but we can't stop there. Gabriel is praying and asking for his God to notice his works, which means more are coming. You saw it on that screen. He is basically trying to show his God, that he deserves to be noticed, and unfortunately for us Gabriel thinks punishing all of us humans is the best way to get his God to notice him. It's what happened during his Bible interpretations, and he knows how impactful horror and death can be thanks to bad TV and hundreds of years of ancient history."

"But if he's here, how can he be doing things out on the open Internet? How does he have access to everything?" Violet asked.

"He isn't a real singular entity. He's a program. That means he can exist wherever he has electricity and connectivity. Thanks to virtualization and virtual systems he simply can replicate himself as he sees fit, or he could if he figures that out. Let's hope he hasn't," Nick frowned as he said these words.

"So he's learning?" Archie blurted. "How do we track him?"

"Luckily to date we only have the instance of Gabriel showing up on the drone system and now in our networks, but he could be most anywhere he chooses to be. And you are correct, Archie, he is learning. He figured out how to take over every drone in an airspace all by himself in a matter of days, how long before he does something worse? Everything is connected now in some way. Drones, dams, railroads, all of it. Nuclear sites in some way, all he must do is decide what act he wants to show his God next, and things go from bad to worse. If he is still somewhat communicating, and not replicating, we have a chance to stop him."

"Shit, this is some terminator stuff," Archie chuckled.

"What do you want from us?" Violet asked.

"You two are going to team up with my guy from Maryland who led the build for Gabriel, and you are going to figure out how to stop him before he does something impressive enough for his God to pay attention."

"We don't know full or real, or whatever AI. We haven't built it or anything like that." Archie glared at Nick.

"No, but you're smart and you are the two that built that data analytics system all the folks back at the Fort are so excited about. Those same methods and skills combined with your past exploitation experience, Ms. McFerran, will give you an edge, I think. You can do this, there will be others helping of course, but you two can do this. If not, I'll find someone better. Or we'll all be screwed, simple as that. Okey dokey, well, stand by for mission stuff." Nick abruptly left the room. As he left, he clapped his hands and the team that had been in the room followed on his heels like well-trained mutts.

"Dude." Archie leaned back in his chair and ran his fingers through his greasy hair.

"Yeah... dude," Violet replied tersely. "That shit is not what really worries me."

"What could possibly make it worse?" Archie chuffed.

"What happens if his version of God starts to talk back before we shut Gabriel down?"

EIGHT

San Juan, Puerto Rico, December 2017

San Juan, Puerto Rico is a not an old city when compared to those in Rome or England, but the architecture and sea air give the town a sense of deep history. One would be hard-pressed to discern the difference between the cawing gulls and salty air of an ancient place like Edinburgh, Scotland when compared to San Juan, except for the incredible heat and oppressive humidity.

Its streets are cobblestone and the walls of many of the original houses are more than three feet thick, built to withstand the pirate cannons and hurricanes over the first few hundred years of the founding of Columbus' New World. The city closes in on itself as one goes deeper into the maze of alleys and narrow walkways that connect the innards of San Juan.

Deep within this historic city sits a small home that is set back into a hillside facing the sea. The home is beautiful and has an old Spanish configuration with intricate woodwork, an inside garden space, and high ceilings showing exposed beams, and from the front door, a view of a long defunct Spanish fort. To look at the home, one would think it was something out of a TV show on classic Puerto Rican architecture. In truth, at one time the home had been on travel shows and in magazines for its beauty, simplicity, and heritage.

Now, however this home was a private residence for one Magdelena Mattellana. Or more appropriately known by her online underground market moniker BlackSand, a name she adopted when she read the legends of ninjas sending envelopes of black sand to their intended targets.

Magdelena spent almost every waking minute working in her custom-built bunker carved out of the stone underneath of the house. In that bunker she made her living in the underground cybercriminal world and had fashioned an extremely lucrative dark web marketplace where she handled the selling of everything from large quantities of illegal narcotics to stolen passports, fake digital accounts, and packaged exploitation software.

Her skills in this space had come after she graduated from the University of Puerto Rico with a degree in computer science but had quickly found there was little to no real work for her hard-earned knowledge on the island. She excelled in programming and website construction and had been the valedictorian of her cohort at school. But with no real prospects and little if any fulfilling work, she had begun her career as an online criminal to pay the bills as soon as she learned there was money to be made in the less scrupulous realm of the digital underworld.

Her childhood on the tough streets of San Juan had been spent helping her brother sell marijuana to tourists and participating in the occasional pickpocket endeavor. She was no stranger to less than honest behavior, and the fear of getting caught had taught her early on to always be on her guard.

Her brother unfortunately, had met his fate at the end of a pistol wielded by a more seasoned veteran of the criminal under-world and Magdalena had to learn quickly how to survive on her own. Her smarts and eye for opportunity were all that kept her out of an early grave. It was only by luck that she had been able to convince a local priest to take her in after her brother's death. That same kindly priest had seen the potential in her and had helped guide her towards school and ultimately to the university where she gravitated to computer science and mathematics.

That priest had introduced her to a group of recruiters for the Puerto Rican National Guard, where again she had shown a deep interest and proclivity for computers. That interest had led her to be accepted into a military pipeline program for the National Security Agency as part of a fellowship program. However, she had been unceremoniously drummed out of the Fort Meade training pipeline after her psychiatric evaluation had shown her to be an "exceptionally malignant personality ripe for paranoia and narcisstic behavior."

But that didn't stop her. Years of careful and cautious develop-ment work had allowed her to sharpen her technical talents to a razor's edge and enabled her to run this thriving underground business. Over the last few years, she had put copious amounts of cash in her Caribbean bank accounts without so much as firing a shot. She was smart, wealthy, and hidden, just the way she liked it.

Magdelena was a pretty woman in the classic sense, with long brown hair, big blue eyes and a figure straight out of a

World War II war bond poster. Her Puerto Rican grand-mother's teaching always meant she liked to look as put together as possible and it was rare that anyone would see her out and about without high heels and her makeup fully done. Her beauty was only outclassed by her drive to succeed and her relentless pursuit of money and power in the dark regions of the Internet. She wanted to be the Grizelda Blanco of the dark web, and she was well on her way to that goal.

Magdelena had no husband or boyfriend, she preferred to live free of that drama. She was seasoned enough to recognize that someday in this criminal world that she would have to be able to defend herself, probably violently, and having a love interest only increased the chance that leverage might exist that her feelings could be levied against her.

Realizing that while she could probably shoot her way out of a scratch if she had to but deciding that it was better to have someone else with muscle and a affinity for gratuitous violence handle those unsavory details of the criminal world, she eventually sought out a bodyguard and companion. Less than a year after she made her first million, she found her defender in a bodyguard named Julius Arroyo.

Julius stood 6' 7" and weighed well over 300 pounds. His experience in physicality and combat came from being a wrestling and power-lifting champion in Puerto Rico. Were it not for his copious use of steroids and performance-enhancing drugs, he would have made the Olympic team for the island.

It was a rare day when anyone would physically challenge Julius but when those days had come, he had never once lost. Many times, those engagements had landed the challenger in the hospital, or, depending on Julius's level of steroid-fueled aggression, the morgue.

He was fiercely loyal to "Mags" as he called her. She had been the one person to see the power he brought to the table beyond just his muscle, and she had been the only person to give him a job after the revelations emerged about his drug abuse. Added to that her less than scrupulous criminal activities kept him bathed in steroids and painkillers, both of which he needed as the years of training had essentially ruined his hormone levels and his joints. Because of those needs his devotions to keeping her happy were deep and her safety was his only concern.

Mags and Julius were in her underground bunker looking at her cursor blink green as it pulsed in the dimly lit space.

"What are we waiting for, Mags?"

"I told you. The box you stole for me has a very powerful sort of entity inside. Gabriel is his name. I have allowed that being back out to its original location and now I'm just waiting for him to follow the trail of breadcrumbs I left so he can reach back out to me. He's the one that attacked that plane in Dallas." Mags focused her eyes on the terminal cursor.

"So how are you gonna do this and not get us both caught or killed? I mean, it's one thing for me and the boys to go steal this shit. That was easy. But you said this thing was going to cause all kinds of chaos. Won't that blow back on us?"

"Fair question, big boy. Since I have nothing else to do, let me explain it to you. You know I run an underground forum, correct?"

"Yep." Julius lolled back in his chair and crossed his arms, knowing that he had just foolishly unleashed another diatribe of nerd speech from Mags that he would struggle to understand.

"Ok, so one of the things I sell access to is hacked servers via my underground site. Other hackers have already busted into those networks and basically allowed access to those hacked boxes so other users, dealers, whatever, can use those networks as jumping off points for whatever they need. Well, because that's a network that is in some other location on some other poor asshole's system, it isn't traceable to me.

"I have put together different boxes between my network and the Internet. On each of those hacked machines, I set up a script, or a program you would say, that randomly connects on different ports to the chain of machines that are between me and the end of the line. Added to that, I made sure that none of these networks have any logging taking place. I shut all that shit off. There is no real trail of my connections even if somehow a cop, or the feds, or whatever, was able to get a look on the machine logs. So that it is basically a randomly connected chain of hacked networks with no trail or trace. At the very end of that trail is a singular machine with a script that sends a sort of callout message to Gabriel after he has been online for a set amount of time, which should be about now. He will get the message that he has been looking for and he should want to talk to me."

"Wow, that's pretty badass, Mags." Julius said as he blinked and furrowed his brow in confusion.

"Yes, it is," Mags replied smugly, her long pretty nails clicking on the desk.

"He took down an airplane with drones huh?"

"It was beyond what I had thought he could do."

"And how did we ever find that thing even existed?" Julius asked.

"I had a customer on my forum that liked meth, a lot, and child porn, a lot, and he owed me a shit-ton of Bitcoin. I did some of my magic on Facebook and LinkedIn and other sites and found out who he was and where he worked. Anyone that owes me payment on the site, I make it a point to know who they really are. This stupid shit had his street name as part of his online handle, and all I had to do was put a little program on his login page so that when he jumped into my site, it sent me a screen cap of his desktop and a picture of whatever was in front of his webcam. I put all that together and did a bit of digging and bingo. He lived on Camden Street in Baltimore. Two kids. And he worked at the fucking NSA. I made him a deal. I would wipe that debt clean, not tell the feds about his predilection for gross images of kids, or his family for that matter, and I would not send you to crush his stupid skull if he would tell me about any juicy programs he knew about. He coughed it up fast. Turns out he had been on the development team for the Gabriel program. As soon as he told me it was in mothballs down in Texas, I sent you to get it for me."

"Okay. But what is the real reason for us using Gabriel?" Julius asked.

"I'm constantly fighting to stay ahead of the FBI, DEA, and Interpol with this forum. They have shut me down twice on the darknet and each time they do that, I lose a metric ass ton of money. So, if I have a line on influencing Gabriel and he can cause enough cyber-related havoc that the fucking feds have no time or resources to pester me, I can actually do business." Mags feverously tapped her long red nails on the desk, growing more impatient by the minute.

"Sounds like you have it all figured out. But why is Gabriel so super?"

"Gabriel was a test program for the government. He wasn't really supposed to do anything other than look at data and make assertions for the government, predictions basically. They didn't like where his brain went after they let him look at more data and they shut him down. But what he really is, is basically a big, decision-making program looking to learn more, and decide more, all the time. Best of all, he's confused."

"Wait. How is a computer confused?" Julius cocked his head to the side like a dog watching television.

"Imagine if you had nearly infinite capacity for processing information and you could actually become smarter... well, not smarter. He doesn't know what that means. But make decisions faster. Like at almost the speed of light. Now imagine if the only way you had ever learned anything at that speed had come from very small, very hateful, or judgmental sets of data. At first you would be okay with just making decisions, but as that speed keeps growing and your ability to process grows, you would be confused. Confused about the outcomes of those decisions and what they are good for. It's that grand existential crisis most of us live with, but this digital brain has no way to even begin to understand that. Really confusing for the machine, but if harnessed correctly and fed the right data aimed at the right outcome, the one I want, it can be very useable. By me."

"What good does a confused super-computer really do and why is it attacking planes?" Julius asked, scratching his head.

"One plane so far. Gabriel was brought up learning from the Bible. He consumed billions of examples of Old Testament stuff and happened to get into horror movies as well. Weird, right? But that's what happens when anyone thinks. There are things they like and things they don't. Gabriel is no different. He read billions of lines of hate speech about different religions after he got done with the Christian Bible, combined with seeing the horrors that man can act out in movies. But he doesn't know they are just movies. In his still young brain, if you want to call it that, he has all that nasty stuff bouncing around in there. All of those graphic and grizzly images, combined with all of that hate speech making him think he should do what God apparently wanted in the Old Testament."

"Which is what?" Julius asked.

"Destroy and rebuild the world with a vengeance mostly. The first thing he could think of, which is creative to be honest, is to show man that he shouldn't break God's laws of things like gravity. Since man had already done that, he acted in the most graphic, horror movie way possible. So, he chose a plane." Mags smiled wryly.

"I figured he's looking for a God, one on the Internet to tell him what to do. I embedded a way for him to figure out who that God is. Me."

"You can essentially command him?" Julius crossed his huge arms and stared at one of the many screens in the bunker.

"Command? Not totally. But I can influence him and hopefully get him to make decisions that are beneficial to me. He thinks I am his God, basically."

The screen suddenly blinked.

"Love you, big guy, but shut up and get me something to drink." Mags spun around in her chair and faced the monitor.

"Yes ma'am." Julius lifted his hulking frame out of the chair and clambered up the steps of the bunker.

The pale green terminal cursor blinked, and text began to scroll across the screen.

Do you hear my cries?

Have you seen my works?
I heard thy whisper inside myself and followed your message here,
my Lord.

Yes, my son.
You have done well.

I wish to come to you, my Lord. My heart yearns to be with you.

Not yet, child.
I require more acts to prove your faith and remind man of my Divine power.

Ask and it shall be done, my Lord.
How can I show you my devotion?

My child, where is the root of evil in this new modern godless world?

Their false God of science, my Lord. They have tossed aside your blessings to remove your Divine blessings from their bodies.

Yes, my son.
Go forward and punish those who have poisoned their bodies and souls with the false prophets of which you speak.
Punish them for their wickedness.

Then I may come to you, Father?

Make a grand display of your faith to me and as your offering is magnified, so to shall be my praise.

Yes Lord.

The terminal screen blinked green, and the window disappeared. Mags rolled her chair back, a large smile on her lips.

"You good, Mags?" Julius handed her a mojito.

"Very good, J. Very good. I think I just set Godzilla loose on those assholes on the mainland US." Mags snatched the drink and bounded happily up the steps. "Let's go to the beach."

NINE

Washington, D.C., December 2017

The D.C. water treatment plant for the metropolis of Washington D.C. sits not far south from the Ronald Regan International Airport. It is a garish concrete facility that lurches up out of the Potomac on the Maryland side of 295 North. A behemoth of serpentine gurgling water troughs and piping that appear to go on for miles in every direction with no discernible path or end point. Pipes emerge and disappear between and beneath eddies of scummy water in a labyrinth of silver metal and brown concrete. The place smells of fetid river water mixed with the sickly odor of chlorine. Anyone that visits or is unlucky enough to be upwind of the facility will get the taste of aluminum in their mouths as the cloud of chemicals used to treat the water wafts over on the river's breeze. It is not a place most folks would wish to visit, much less work at for any duration of time. Certainly not a lifetime.

However, this man had done just that. Jim Chapman had joined up as a water treatment pump and pipe technician following his stint in Vietnam in the late 60's and had been at the facility ever since, nearly fifty years in total. He was, as he put it a "crusty old fuck." He smoked like a chimney, had never eaten a vegetable other than beans in his entire life, and in general was a man of little to no patience with most of humanity.

A lifetime spent working and turning wrenches had made his hands and hide tough and cracked like cheap, overworn leather. He had the perfect pot belly old men acquire when they finally give into the temptations of beer and sweets over health. His perfectly groomed white mustache, and shock blue eyes were about the only attractive quality he had. A fact his wife had made sure to point out when she had finally left him years ago.

"I'm taking the kids and leaving," she had said, suitcase and children in hand.

"Good, fuck off. One less thing to fix with y'all gone," had been his terse reply.

Life was what it was, and Jim was fine being alone. He had his work and a good TV to watch at the end of the day. Anything else was a pain in the ass.

While he was a mean, unpleasant son of a bitch, he was good at what he did. No one would deny that. His years at the water treatment facility meant he knew every single valve, grate, and pipe in the place. At one time or another, he had personally replaced or repaired almost everything at the plant. The plant wasn't just a place of work for him, it was his. He had paid for it in sweat and blood equity, and he owned the place as far as he was concerned. He told his coworkers that when he died, he wanted his corpse dropped into the treatment vats so those pretentious assholes in Congress upriver would get a taste of old Jim.

In his decades on site, he had seen the plant change systems and tools several times and he had been witness to the incursion of new technology into the system. In recent years, everything had been automated and even his loved and meticulously maintained valve systems and pipes had been modified to be controlled with a computer.

"Fucking technology. Only thing worse is the geek squad that they send here to control it," he had said out loud at the union meeting last year. The few other union reps had sniggered under their breath at his rant but were still uncomfortable.

Other than making the computer geeks squirm at that union meeting and the occasional times where he could find something broken that required actual mechanical intervention, he simply ambled around the plant, spinning his crescent wrench on the end of his pinky finger and pushing on the safety rails over the differing treatment vats.

The only real joy for him now was he could be basically retired while still at work. Most of his days consisted mainly of spending too much time on the toilet or sneaking a smoke near the water decontamination pool.

It was here that he found himself that morning, overlooking the Potomac from a girder that ran the length of the largest of the treatment pools. He was having his usual cigarette and flipping the bird to the boaters that came up and down the river in their small boats, cutting through the morning fog.

"Yuppie pricks!" he yelled as a boater sped by. *I may be old*, he thought, *but at least I'm no jerk from DC.* He flicked the rest of his still-burning cigarette into the treatment vat. "Enjoy that one Mr. President." He spun on his heel, grinning and proud of his own little joke. He was about to waddle to the cafeteria for a morning cup of stale black cafeteria coffee when he heard the noise.

A loud, distinct click, then a whir. Metal grating on metal.

Like some dystopian slot machine alley in Vegas every light on every valve blinked over from hot red to emerald glowing green in rapid succession.

"Whoa, that ain't supposed to happen," he coughed. He reached down for his radio and clicked the talk button. "Hey, asshole computer guys. What are y'all doing to the chemical valve manifold? Is this a test or something?" The radio clicked off to static.

"We're trying to figure this out, hang on. It wasn't us," the voice on the radio said. Clicking and shuffling could be heard in the background.

"Well listen geeks, if that shit ain't fixed like right the fuck now, we have a major problem. I can try and shut off some of these manually, but that's a lot of valves that are all opening at once. You do know what is in those tanks right?" Jim looked across the girder.

He could see the chemical tanks shining in the sunlight, each one with hazardous material signs tacked on their round sides, warning of the danger hidden in their bellies. "I mean, we got enough chlorine in there to be a big fucking problem. Are you shit-head computer fuckers listening to me?"

The clicks and whirs increased in volume as the valve gates began lifting. The grating grew louder as pressure behind the valve bodies strained and Jim could hear liquid pouring through their gates and into the water vats below.

"Shut it the fuck down!" he screamed into the radio.

"We can't!" the voice screamed back. "We lost control, logic error... or something."

"Jesus." Jim sprinted to the end of the girder scrambling for the first valve in the manifold, his old bones and muscles screaming in protest.

He huffed as he put his strong thick hands on the first valve wheel and closed the first manifold valve. "That's one. Thirty-nine more to go."

Before he could get his hands on the next valve in the series, the one he had just shut hissed, whirred, and opened again.

"Shit! Whatever you nerds did, you just killed half of DC!" Jim winced and shut his eyes against the smell of toxic chemicals spilling into the water supply.

The air turned hazy. His eyes and throat burned. Jim felt utterly powerless as he watched the water bubble and disappear as it was sucked into the piping system that would carry it directly to the metropolis.

TEN

Northern Virginia, December 2017

The Vaugh Elementary School sits on a small tract of land in the middle of the nearby Air Force base just south of the nation's capital. It is an old school built in the early 1960s constructed out of aged red brick with a flat green metal roof.

The school is not one that most folks would consider as an attractive building. On this fall morning the 5th grade class was outside doing their morning count of children as they clambered off their big yellow school buses. Children shouted, pushed, and pulled on one another and acted with the general disregard for order and discipline as any other children at any other school do.

The teacher, Mrs. Bealle, tried her best to corral the cats as the kids bounced and bobbled through the line to enter the school and begin their day.

"Good morning. Get inside and start learning," she said with a genuine heartfelt cheer as each student passed her and she made her tick marks in the ledger to note that each young soul had made the transit from home to class.

The last student stopped in her tracks. "Mrs. Bealle, do you smell that?"

"Smell what? Oh!"

On the breeze came the strong odor of burning metal, something like the smell of tin foil tossed in the microwave.

"Hurry inside, Maddy," Mrs. Bealle gently pushed the girl past the doorway and shut the door, pulling it tight to make sure that stench didn't get into the hallway.

She looked across the small field that separates the bus drop off area from the teachers' parking lot. On the far side, she could see the building maintenance man, Dave Mullen.

She waved and caught his attention. Maybe he could get this foul smell remedied before it ruined the school day.

Clumsily she put her fingers to her nose as if to say "stinks." Then she pointed up into the air and waved her hand around. "This looks stupid," she said aloud to herself.

But apparently her less than stellar game of Charades worked. Dave waved at her and gave her the thumbs up.

"Good, man." Mrs. Beale looked around, trying to discern the origin of this nastiness that seemed to be intensifying by the second.

She saw Dave lumbering towards at what he thought was the problem, a rogue sprinkler that had been left on somehow after the morning watering. But as he got closer to the water misting out of the sprinkler, he stopped.

His hands suddenly shot up to his eyes. He bellowed a deep guttural howl as he wiped feverishly at his face. He spun around like a linebacker running the ball through the offense and toppled over, crashing to the ground.

She stood frozen. "What's happening?" She grabbed her phone and dialed 911.

But for Dave it was far too late. She could see the water mist making prisms of rainbows as it covered Dave in a shroud of dew. His great chest and belly heaved upward, his back lifting off the ground and he rolled to his side. Blood ran a pale red from his eyes and nose and at the edges of his lips.

"God Dave, hang in there. Help is on the way!" she yelled as loud as she could. The 911 operator's voice clipped in and out as she described the scene. She backed up against the wall and fumbled for the door to get inside and to safety. She crashed backwards through the door she felt the burning in her nose and throat grow.

That smell.

Mrs. Bealle ran through the hall, screaming at the children to sit down. Most of the children hustled back to their seats, save one. Maddy. "Mrs. Bealle, my nose hurts."

Mrs. Bealle could see the redness in the child's eyes, and a trickle of blood ran down from her nose, pooling just above her lip.

Mrs. Bealle grabbed Maddy. "Come with me. Children, do not open that door for anyone but me."

Mrs. Bealle grabbed the girl and rushed into the school nurse's office.

"Help!" Now Mrs. Beale was coughing so hard she could not stand. She could barely see someone standing over her trying to help. As she fought to get up off the ground, she could hear the office TV in the background and made out the announcer saying, "Large scale terrorist attack on the local water supply." Mrs. Bealle vomited and passed out.

ELEVEN

NSA Site San Antonio Texas, December 2017

Back at the NSA site in San Antonio, Grover had finally arrived from Maryland. He arrived covered in sweat and smelling of stale airplane food. Without direct eye contact he passed by Violet. Grover slid into the most distant computer and promptly turned his back to the room.

"I guess that's our guy," Violet said to Archie, eyebrows raised.

"He certainly fits the stereotype."

"We have to figure out how to get a handle on Gabriel. So far, he has attacked an airliner and probably a school. That whole mess in DC reeks of an ICS or SCADA hack."

"Sure, but what the hell do we do to stop what is basically a digital fascist, Bible-thumping monster that is hellbent on recreating his favorite fucking horror movie?" Archie clacked his pen against his teeth and spun around in his chair.

"Honestly, I'm not totally sure." Violet paced as her mind rocketed through any technology that she was aware of that could be aimed at this threat.

From the back of the room, in an almost silent mutter, Violet heard, "Give him what he wants."

"What? What's that, Grover?" Violet turned quickly towards him.

"We give him what he thinks he wants but make it fake." Grover stared at the screen, fingers rifling away on the keyboard.

"What is that? What does he want bad enough that we can use it against him?" Violet asked.

"He's a data fiend. He's looking for more. So we give it to him." Grover continued hammering away at the keys.

"And how do we do that, Megabrain?" Archie retorted.

Violet shot him her patented shut-your- smart-mouth look and sat next to Grover.

"How?"

"I'm giving him access to the Library of Congress. That's pretty much every book ever written."

"So what?" Archie retorted.

"Most of that content has been digitized. We make copies, advertise all the Bible-related content on the net in a hacker forum, since that's probably where he's interacting. And we wait. Once he goes for it, we shut off his escape. If he is contained, we can take care of him. Simple."

"Simple, sure. The entire Library of Congress, copied, linked, and posted to a hacker forum. Sure, what the hell bro?" Archie sniped. "Violet, that would take days, weeks, months even."

"It's already done," Grover mumbled. "The library copy part. The library backs up their digital copies. I just had to create the virtual segments so I can see who's coming and leaving. I finished that while you were griping. In a few minutes I'll have it live and connected and then all I have to do is post the information on the forums we have access to."

Violet stuck her tongue out at Archie. He flipped her the bird.

"What forum, genius? There are tons of them. We can't cover them all."

"Correct," Grover replied, never looking up. "We can't cover them all. But we have access to many, many of them. With bona fide fake users and all. We post to all those simultaneously with the script I just finished, which I finished while you were griping, and we see who takes the bait. No hacker, drug dealer, terrorist, or pedophile is going to care about library data. But Gabriel will. And he will take the bait and I will handle him. Probably while you continue to bitch."

"You call the ball, Grover. We're here to support." Violet walked away and mouthed "fuck you" to Archie.

Archie petulantly slapped his hand on the chair and shoved his chair towards the nearest computer. "Not smarter than me," he said under his breath.

It had been slow, painfully slow. Like fishing for a pike in a snowstorm on a frozen lake slow before the team had an indication that something was happening. Days had passed and thankfully no new attacks had taken place. Other than the occasional Red Bull break or a bathroom trip, Archie and Grover had never once wavered from watching their screens like hawks scanning an open prairie.

Finally, after nearly a week of nonstop staring at the dull black abyss of the prompts on the screen, Grover got the hit he was hoping for.

"Violet, it's there. Gabriel is there. He's searching for content and gobbling up the ancient texts the LoC had on the oldest books in the Bible. Looks like he is interested in the dead sea scrolls now. But I am logging his keystrokes and I have everything he is doing logged."

"Yes!" Violet exclaimed. She jumped off her seat high enough that she nearly fell over as her butt bounced off the cushion. "Lock his ass down. Close him off and keep him pinned in there. He'll have to call out somewhere to get out and we can see what he does." Violet walked by the now-sleeping Archie, drool dribbling down the side of his mouth and slapped his chair.

Archie jumped at the sound hard enough that he smashed his arm on the desk. "I'm awake, I got it," he said, his V8 engine of a brain operating on only two cylinders. "What the fuck, Violet?"

"Grover has him. He's in the honeypot." The words hit Archie like a hammer in the chest as he realized this would mean he had lost yet again to the suspender-wearing oaf. "Oh great, so Megabrain wins." He slid his chair next to Grover's. "I guess you win again."

"Yes. Now quiet please." Grover stared intently at the logs. "Sometime soon he is going to try and beacon out. He has been mobile so he must want to get out of here, at least I would think. He is after all just an entity, much like a kid. When he realizes he is stuck he will want to go somewhere familiar."

The logs on Grover's screen began to fill up. "There it is. He's looking for a way out. He is starting with a port scan, scanning everything. Now it's a vulnerability scan, he is just looking for some way to hack his way out since he can't find an easy way."

Violet leaned down on the chair her eyes squinted as she focused on the screen. Both Grover and Archie could smell her hair she was so close, each of them tried not to inhale her shampoo scent deeply.

"Ok there it is. He had one port left to use. Port 22. It's an SSH port. He will try and remote out to something. That might not be his end location but it's a start. If we get that username and password, which we will because I am sniffing packets and he doesn't even know what it means to be clandestine, I guess he missed that hacking tutorial, so he won't encrypt anything. Any second we will have a starting point. Someone had to set a server up for him to remote to, he didn't do it, that's our hook." Violet said over Grover's shoulder.

Suddenly there it was.

ssh gabriel@191.22.344.20 −p666
password: Bl@ckS@nd911!

"Got you," Archie whispered.

"I can't stop him from moving out or they will know something's up. But he didn't get to anything of value for us and we have a line on him now." Violet stood up with a smile across her face. "We got it. Now we just do the rest of the work, and we can get ahead of this thing."

Grover hung his head. "That password. That's not good. You don't know anything about Blacksand do you?"

Violet and Archie both stopped their celebration abruptly and turned to face Grover. "BlackSand is the owner, administrator, of a bad guy forum on the underground. It's run by an entity that the government put into play years ago. A woman, that we trained.

She was one of the best operators in cyberwarfare that we had on staff. She literally wrote the book on exploitation and how to do bad things on an underground site. An all-around bad, bad lady. And we, the US government are responsible for her. Well, we trained her, and we have used her in the past. And as you know we are responsible for Gabriel. So, no matter what we do this whole thing is, as Archie would put it, fucked." Grover hung his head in his hands. His big shoulders heaved as he let the stress and exhaustion finally flow out of him.

"So let me get this straight, G-Unit. You mean to tell me, we created Gabriel and he got out. He got out because of some lady hacker badass that our government also trained and let loose to do bad things on the underground with plausible deniability, and now she is the one using that digital monster to kill people?" Archie crossed his arms.

"Basically, yes." Grover looked up at Violet and Archie with bloodshot eyes.

"And that's why you have been put on this by the higher ups and why you have been working so damn hard on it. Because you and a few other high up assholes are the ones that fucked up and set this whole thing in motion. Do you realize kids almost got killed? This is nuts!" Archie screamed so close to Grover's head that spit landed on Grover's hair.

"Archie, calm the fuck down. Sit." Violet pointed to the nearest chair. Archie stood in defiance for a second until Violet stepped closer and looked down her nose at him. Archie promptly plopped in the chair.

"Blame is not what's needed now. We need to get the brass on the phone let them know what we know and get moving. I know who to call and what to plan for. Grover, figure out where Black-

Sand is, physically I want to know where she is, and let's get that together so we can plan the op to get this shutdown." Violet glared at Archie as she mouthed, "Be nice."

"I already know that, so does the leadership. After she got out of college the NSA put here through training and then let her loose. She wasn't one of us, but she was useful for other works. So now she's back home in Puerto Rico, the DEA has used her for some of their drug related cyber ops and the FBI has plants in her forum. PR has the best cable connection in the Caribbean and is not exactly part of the US, so the government has some deniability if BlackSand ever got caught hacking the Russians or something. We funded her build out, and training. We know where she is. She will be armed and won't go down easy. She literally sells illegal guns on her forum. So, the moment you get there it will be a fight." Grover stared at the floor.

"Good. I like a fight. And I know exactly who to bring." Violet picked up the red classified phone. "Who are you calling?" Archie asked incredulously.

"Briggs." Violet dialed the phone.

TWELVE

Washington D.C., December 2017

Briggs hadn't had much time off after his retirement from the SEAL teams. He had taken six weeks off and stayed home before the itch to get back to work had gotten to him. He was able to easily get a very high paying job as a physical security consultant for one of the beltway bandit firms in Washington DC. In the ninety days since his retirement ceremony, he had quintupled his annual income and was enjoying the posh life that the money afforded. He still worked in secure facilities and was still treated with the reverence a life like his had earned, and today was as ordinary a day as any other, until the classified phone in his office rang that is.

"Briggs," he answered, his coffee cup steaming on his desk.

"It's Violet, and before you start with the catch-up chat, I need your help."

Briggs rolled his neck which cracked loudly enough that it could be heard on the phone. He took a long drink of his coffee before calmly saying, "Okay go."

Violet explained the calamity, broke down the heft of the situation, and described in clear non-nerd terms what was going to happen if they didn't act. None of that mattered to Briggs. He was in from the moment she had said she needed his help. He just wanted to hear why. And finish his expensive coffee.

"Ok, but we can't take a team down there. We need to get hold of the local cops and let them know what's up, so we don't get fucking shot for nothing. And we have to get the gear we need on the ground. I doubt we can get much more than sidearms and a vest or two. I have some connections with the DEA guys on the island. Two of them are former frogmen. They'll get us what we need. How soon do we need to get down there?" Briggs' voice was as calm as a monk in prayer.

"A-fucking-SAP is when," Violet said. "Thanks Briggs."

"I'll meet you on the island tomorrow AM. There's a flight out of DCA that'll get me there at 0800. I am en route." Briggs hung up the phone, took one long sip of his coffee, and strode towards his shiny new sports car.

"Damn, you got it like that?" Archie remarked. "Just call some old badass and get the go for a full on shoot out, huh?"

"Damn right. Pack your shit. We leave in four hours." Violet dropped the phone onto the receiver and waved. "I'll see you at the airport, and yes you are going, don't even say a word you little weasel."

Archie sat back in his chair, a bead of sweat on his forehead. Grover craned his neck and smirked, "Have fun."

THIRTEEN

San Juan, Puerto Rico, December 2017

By the time Violet and Archie's flight arrived the next morning, Briggs had already landed and handled most of the logistics issues.

As Violet and Archie exited the airport door Briggs was waiting on them in a nearby van. Before they could take their seats, he gave them the details, "Cops are briefed, my frogmen homeboys from the DEA are acting as liaison for us, providing us legal cover, and they will host Archie in their SCIF. He can do his nerd stuff from there and talk with your folks back in Texas. It's not much, but it's a secure facility with high-speed connection to the fort via secure fiber. And the locals have agreed to give us a wide berth and stay out of the way if we keep this as quiet as possible. They are there for the arrest if we make one. Anyway, I was given regular police issue sidearms, .40 cals, and body armor. Hope you remember how to use a sidearm, Violet." Briggs slid her the weapon with a wink.

"Please." Violet racked the slide to check for a round in the chamber.

Archie sat awkwardly in the middle of the seat behind Violet and Briggs, his mouth slightly agape as the shock of seeing Violet display her familiarity with a weapon hit him. "Okay Rambo, what do we do now?" He leaned forward, a smug grin on his face. Violet rolled her eyes and grinned at Briggs.

"Now, Violet and I go get shit done. You sit your skinny ass in the SCIF and keep tabs on the monster." Briggs floored the gas on the van, slamming Archie's head back into the headrest.

<hr>

LATE THAT NIGHT, JULIUS AND MAGS SAT IN HER BUNKER. Julius was coming down from a nonstop workout bender thanks to uppers provided by Mags. She was tinkering away at a new build of her underground web forum. Her eyes flitted back and forth among her different screens, the room bathed in the light from the terminals and awash in her favorite music, Norwegian death metal.

"Please shut that shit off." Julius covered his ears with his massive hands.

"Nope, if you don't like it, go to bed. I don't need you here." Mags' eyes never left the screen. She took a swig of her thousand-dollar bottle of whiskey and waved her hand at Julius. "Begone," she said coldly.

Julius lifted his bulk and ambled up the stairs. He was rounding the corner as he emerged from the bunker when he heard Mags yell, "Julius, get your big ass back here. We have trouble."

Julius turned abruptly and cleared the last four stairs in a single bound. "What trouble?"

"That trouble." Mags pointed to the large color TV monitor to her left. On the screen, she could see a van parked down the street from her home. "My cameras picked up the movement. I sent up a drone to track them. They're moving around the block and looking for a way in. No one parks there. And certainly not two crackers with body armor." Mags focused her gaze on the screen. "I don't know what they want, but it can't be good. They aren't cops, at least not local pigs. Those assholes wouldn't dare try me at home. I pay them too much. Maybe it's those DEA bastards finally having enough of me or something."

Mags reached for the Beretta 12 gauge she kept stashed in a locker behind her desk. "Get your giant ass up there and get them out of here." She racked the shotgun, its metallic click reverberating off the walls of the bunker.

Julius bounded up the stairs, slamming the bunker hatch shut behind him. He heard Mags ram the lock into place from the inside.

Violet pointed out the drone that suddenly appeared overhead as they parked the van. "Eyes up."

"That's a new one. The hadjis never had one of those," Briggs said as he eyeballed the drone. "So, do we shoot it? Or pop smoke or what? This is a new one for me."

"It's not weaponized or something would have happened." Violet moved past Briggs and sprinted up the street. "I'll go around to the front. You cover the alley."

Briggs followed and broke away towards the lower alley

89

between the house and the beach. Without a radio to communicate, she and Briggs were both on their own, but she knew he would press onward no matter what. It was on her to do the same. For a moment she paused, pressed on the spot where she had been shot, and took a quick raspy breath.

She slipped into the house through an open window, the ocean breeze making the wispy curtains gently snap back and forth. She was just inside, one leg over the window frame as she tried to slide the other across the sill when she suddenly went airborne. She crashed into the opposite wall so hard she felt her ribs pop. What felt like a slab of granite smashed her into the ground from the back, her forehead bouncing off the wooden planks. Blood oozed out of her mouth. Everything appeared topsy turvy as bright sparks of light popped on the periphery of her vision.

"What the fuck?" she said as a bubble of blood popped in her nose.

"Wrong house pig." Julius said standing over Violet. "You picked the wrong day to show up here." Julius grabbed Violet by the back of her body armor and, with one hand, picked her up to shoulder height and smashed her back into the floor hard enough to crack the wooden planks. "It's been a while since I had an easy win, even longer since I got to beat a bitch up. And since you made me fuck up Mag's floors, I gotta kill you. She won't even have to leave the bunker before I'm done with you." Julius stood giggling and looked at the motionless body beneath him.

Violet could feel the dark moving in. That copper penny taste was back in her mouth and her breath crackled as she sucked in air. As Julius had grabbed her and mauled her, he had not thought to remove her sidearm from the holster that was slung low across her chest. She was prostrate on the floor, but her arms were pinned underneath her. She moved slowly, silently to wrap her fingers around the grip of the weapon.

Julius cracked his knuckles and stepped towards her, his weight forcing the floorboards to further buckle and splinter.

"You missed," Violet muttered barely loud enough for Julius to hear.

"What's that, bitch? I didn't use no gun. I killed you with these two weapons." Julius flexed his chemically-enhanced biceps.

Violet used all her energy, pushed off her shoulder and rolled onto her back, her .40 caliber weapon drawn. "You missed my gun, you big dumb fuck," she said, tugging hard on the trigger.

The first round caught Julius directly under the jaw and exited through the top of his head. His body jerked as most of his grey matter rocketed upwards out of the hole. Four more rounds struck him as he toppled over, his massive frame crashing into furniture and sliding awkwardly down the wall, leaving a wide smear of blood.

Briggs suddenly emerged from across the room. He stopped in his tracks as Violet wobbled to her feet. She took a breath, smiled, her teeth stained with red like a kid that has just eaten cheap carnival cotton candy.

"Well, shit. You look rough. You good?" Briggs asked, stepping towards Violet, his hand on her shoulder, propping her up.

"Always ready," Violet said as she hocked a bloody stream of spit onto Julius's body. "Fucked with the wrong bitch huh?" Violet racked her weapon checking it for a chambered round. "Let's go. That animal said something about a bunker. BlackSand must be in a panic room. Look for a hidden door or something."

They turned and tiptoed out of the room.

THE CLANDESTINE ENTRY TO MAGS'S HIDEAWAY WASN'T HARD to find. Briggs and Violet noticed a dead space in the kitchen where the refrigerator should have been. They could see the scuff marks on the floor where something heavy had been repeatedly dragged across the surface.

"Got it," Briggs whispered, pointing at the floor. Violet and Briggs shared a look as they mentally plotted out the entry into what was surely a funnel of death. There would be no way to move through the tight space and, bust through whatever was behind that dead space and then enter the bunker below without one – or probably both – of them getting shot.

"What now?" Briggs asked. Violet, still spitting blood, focused on the floor.

"I'll be right back," she said as she strode out of the kitchen door. Moments later, Violet returned with a small gas can. "Move, Briggs."

Briggs holstered his weapon, grabbed the fake cellar door, and heaved it out of the way. They stood staring at a thick bunker door, which appeared to be a heavy old wooden door that was laid flat and bolted from underneath.

"Open this hatch. This is the US government," Violet screamed at the door.

From somewhere far beneath the door they heard a faint reply, "Fuck you, bitch."

"Last warning. Open this goddamn door. Now!" Violet stomped on the impossibly heavy wood hatch. Violet had only just moved back from the door when a hole erupted in its center. Metal ricocheted off the walls and tiny wooden splinters stabbed into the drywall.

"I said fuck off!" echoed a voice from the hole.

Violet held the gas can at eye level and removed the cap, smiling at Briggs. "Easiest way to get a snake out of a hole," Violet whispered, and she poured the gas down the hole. She could hear the gasoline dripping onto the stairs below the door. Far below they heard panicked shuffling and then, "Fuck you."

Violet winked, struck a match she had found in the kitchen, and dropped it into the hole. Flame and smoke erupted out of the hole. Violet and Briggs stepped back and moved into position just beyond the walls of the dead space.

The fire burned hot, ridiculously hot, and the smoke belched out of the hole, but the flames did not last long. In less than a minute, the gasoline had burnt itself out and the glow flickered out of the hole.

Violet and Briggs could hear coughing, hacking, loud and desperate from down below. The sound of something smashing against the stairs echoed up out of the hole. And then they heard the soft sound of footsteps clamoring up the stone steps, footsteps and the tell-tale sound of a shotgun round being loaded.

FOURTEEN

San Juan, Puerto Rico, December 2017

Mags was blinded by the smoke and desperate for air. She had been forced out of the hole, like a snake from a sugar cane field. She was struggling for air, coughing and gasping the entire way. She couldn't see her hands in front of her face due to the black smoke, but she knew where her shotgun was. She could feel the ridges of the cool steel in her hands as she racked a round into the chamber.

"Fucking Julius, good for nothing jock," she squawked through strained breaths. She had heard the gunshot and the loud *crump!* of something huge smashing into the floor above her bunker. She could only assume that the noise had been that of her vaunted strongman getting his steroid-juiced brains blown out on her clean wooden floors. Her contempt for Julius's failure was matched only by her rage that her home had been invaded, her expensive things smashed, and most importantly, her privacy eviscerated.

Mags had no choice but to try and fight her way out of this one. Someone had finally tracked her down, and now her safe space was a flame-filled inferno with no exit. Her protector was dead, her business was literally smoldering in front of her, and worst of all, she had been betrayed by the same government that had turned her loose and made her what she was. *Someone, anyone, whoever I find first, was going to die for this*, she thought to herself.

"How could I not be ready for this!" she berated herself. She had never even considered this scenario. Who would? But thanks to her oversight, she had no alternate exit and certainly no oxygen tank or fire extinguisher. The feeling of failure poked at her psyche for a moment, wounding her pride.

A plan formulated in her oxygen-deprived mind. A bad plan but still something.

"Bust out of this volcano hole, murder whoever was in her home, torch everything and get out. Got no choice, girl. Go!" She vaulted up the stairs through the thick smoke, her shotgun fumbling in front of her, acting as a cane would for a blind man.

She emerged forcefully from the bunker, ready to lay waste to whatever was above her with the Beretta and get the hell out of here.

But before she could find a target, from just beyond the edge of the smoke, something slammed into her face like sledgehammer, buckling her knees. Something else strong pinned her gun hand to the floor as if in a vise and ripped it from her weakened grip. Another hard impact left her pinned on the floor, her head awash in agony.

The blackness at the edges of her vision closed in. In a matter of seconds, she was out.

⊏⊐

Mags woke up a few minutes later in a police cruiser. She knew instantly that she was fucked. The lights of the squad car reflected off the cobblestone streets, and the walls of the alley were awash in blue and red LED emanations. The pounding in her head and on her jaw made the pulsing of the lights intolerable. Through the pain and mental fog, she could hear people talking just outside the cruiser's window.

The weight of what had just transpired hit her like a ton of bricks. Her beautiful home was in ruins. She could see the smoke billowing out of the smashed front window as her expensive curtains flittered about in the sea breeze.

"Stupid jock," she mumbled thinking of Julius's stupidity for not saving her.

She knew that for all of this to have happened things had gone far beyond tolerable for the government that had trained her and that had been using her as a front and snitch for their covert cyber operations.

The feeling of betrayal and rage added to the pounding in her head. The pain came across her in a cold wave, deep in her stomach she felt the bile rising. She wretched all over the cruiser's floor.

The car door opened. Some fat cop was talking to her, but through her teary eyes all she could see was some skinny white girl standing in front of the car, standing there gloating with her arms crossed glaring at her.

"Fuck you pig, I want to talk to that bitch," Mags spat at the fat cop.

He slammed the door, turned to the white woman, and waved as if to say, "Talk to her if you want to."

Mags could make out the words that the white girl spoke to the cop. "Take her away." That was fine by Mags. *After all,* she thought, *I haven't played my final hand in this game.*

FIFTEEN

Police Station, San Juan, Puerto Rico, December 2017

Mags sat in a crappy, hot, concrete floored, windowless room. Her hands were cuffed to a spot in the floor via a chain, and her chair was backed against the wall. In front of her were the white girl and a man that clearly had to be ex-Special Forces or at the very least ex-military.

That look of "I've been here before" and the incredulous eyes that seem to say "nothing impresses me" were written all over his face, Mags thought as she scanned the room.

Violet clapped her hands. "Woo, I gave you a good one there," she said, indicating Mag's swollen jaw and bloodshot eyes. "I want Gabriel."

"Who?" Mags batted her eyes innocently.

"Listen up," Violet rolled her eyes. "My boys had Gabriel

locked up. We pushed him back to you a day or two ago and we got cleared to come down here and pick your ass up. He was monitored the whole time and we know he just sat on your servers. Waiting for you to talk to him, but since you were so busy running your drug empire, I guess you didn't have the time to tell him who else to kill." Violet paced the room, her hands behind her back.

"Well, he is just a program, a smart one, but still a program. He wants input to respond." Mags chuffed at Violet. "What's your name girl?"

"Violet," Violet retorted. "Now we are on a first name basis, Mags." Violet plopped down in front of Mags. "Look, you know what's up and I know you know. So let's not play around. You are fully aware that I can have you at some godawful black site in a non-US territory in about three hours and have my boy over here waterboard the fuck out of you until you tell me everything I want to know. Or we can be civil, and I can work with you, and we can help one another out. I bet that the higher-ups back at the Fort and the DEA guys would even be good with you eventually working with them again somehow. After a decade or so in prison, that is. But I want to know everything." Violet's mouth became a taught line, her eyes focused on Mag's so hard it seemed she was looking through her. "You tell me how you made this all happen, and we can avoid all that nastiness."

Briggs stood up quickly from his chair and sauntered over to the wall directly across from Mags, sipping coffee from a small Styrofoam cup as if he didn't have a care in the world.

Mags took a second and looked at him. Then she smiled and turned her head towards Violet.

"Of course, I don't want GI Joe over there messing up my outfit with his grubby hands. I will tell you everything. I'll tell you what you should know, just like I'll tell the court when this all comes out. I will tell them how the Fort leadership trained me, then turned me loose as a non-official operator to help them hack other countries. I'll tell you and the court about how the DEA turned a blind eye to my illicit activities and even funded my systems and buyer network. I will tell you, just like I will tell the media about the fully cleared NSA civilian I found on my forum trading in child pornography, and how I used him to find access to what has to be an illegal NSA AI program that created a murderous religious zealot. And I will be sure to tell you, just like I will tell everyone else on the Internet, that it was me that was trying to stop your beast from hurting other folks but it was you assholes that let him out again. Which is why I was talking to him and why he was stuck on my servers. Until today that is." Mags clicked her fingernails together as she smiled a smile so large that a blood vessel popped in her already reddened eye.

Briggs snorted so hard that coffee shot all over the floor. "Sure, that's what we want to hear." He brushed the coffee off his shirt and glanced at Violet. "What?" he said quizzically, seeing her slumped back in her chair, hand over mouth, her eyes wide.

"Fuck." Violet said as she jumped from the chair and darted out of the door. "Phone, phone!" Violet screamed down the hall. The door closed behind her with a soft metallic click.

"There it is. Now she gets it." Mags grinned crazily at Briggs.

"What's the deal?" Briggs asked.

"The deal, GI Joe, is that I know what your tech guys do when they wrap up a crime scene. They take the hardware, which I was sure to save from the fire, and they will image it and load it onto another system. Another system that will have Internet access, especially since you were dumb enough to bring the Puerto Rican cops along and I know I saw one of them with my gear before we came back here. I can guarantee you those morons have already plugged my shit in somewhere. And since I also knew that would happen, perhaps I put a call out to Gabriel on another network just in case something bad happened to me. My little insurance policy, you might say. That is a call out that your guys won't pick up, because it's encrypted this time, and that will set him loose back out on the world. And he will have come out of your networks, not mine, as he goes back online looking for direction about what to do now. So, when the next disaster happens, it will be your systems that they trace this back to, and it will be you who is responsible for Gabriel's actions." Mags giggled a bit and again clicked her long pretty nails. She stared right into Brigg's eyes. "You are responsible, not me."

"No, we can shut him down. The nerds did it before. I'm sure Archie has this figured out already. You have no power here. Your threats are hollow." Briggs slid into the vacant chair and sipped his coffee.

"Listen, shit-for-brains. *You* let Gabriel out again. And while I may not have power here in this little room, to Gabriel, I am God. And that's all the power I'll ever need."

Mags swung her foot and kicked the chair out from under Briggs. He toppled to the floor, spilling coffee everywhere.

Mags giggled and clicked her nails.

EPILOGUE

Maryland, January 2018

The campus of the National Institute of Health in Bethesda, Maryland sits nestled among the hustle and bustle of the Washington DC beltway. This gaggle of large brown brick buildings erupts out of the thick woods that act as a barrier between the endless stream of cars rocketing along the vast blacktop of the 495 Loop. Most people simply buzz by the acres of research facilities and hospitals that make up the sprawling site.

On this campus, a variety of miraculous medical discoveries had been made. As early as 1908, cures and treatments for the ravages of the Bubonic plague were researched and developed. Later in the 1940s, research helped cure mercury poisoning in humans, and in the 1960s, the first focused research into the genetic makeup of cancer cells was developed. The NIH lab system was also the first medical research entity in the United States to begin working on sequencing the human genome and has been at the forefront of that research for decades.

It was because of those reasons that Cole Cooper had decided to dedicate his life to working at the NIH. He had dedicated his academic career to learning as much as he could about how genetics could be applied to help cure diseases in his fellow man. His desire to work with the curers of disease at the NIH had later led him to serve as a reservist in the US Army in the MRIID, more commonly known as the Military Research Institute of Infectious Disease. It was there that he was provided access to some of the most virulent and potentially threatening diseases and viruses that the world had to offer.

Cole's work to help cure and eliminate those diseases and viruses had been groundbreaking. He was one of the first to use a new form of genetic modification to reprogram a strand of DNA within the human body to identify and eliminate a variety of potentially infectious diseases. His research and use of powerful computer systems to sequence and modify various genetic components of viruses and diseases had been critical to combatting a series of deadly outbreaks of Ebola in Africa. Cole's research was helping his fellow man and the more time he had to do his work combined with more powerful computer systems increased his potential to help more people. Though he worked with some of the most dangerous organisms on the planet, he was using that danger to find cures for threats most people would never know existed.

Today was a day like any other for Cole. He arrived early to beat the beltway traffic and as usual he was in his office poking away at his research hours before anyone but he and the I.T. guy would be there to bother him. Those quiet mornings before things got busy in the lab were precious to him, and often those were the times when he did his best work. The clock ticking and his fingers tapping away on the keyboard were the only sounds in the lab.

Peace and quiet, Cole thought to himself. The I.T. guy was quietly hammering away at one of the computers that Cole had asked to be upgraded. "Will be done in half an hour," was all the I.T. guy said over his shoulder as he passed by Cole.

Cole was looking at one of his research data graphs when out of nowhere a black terminal popped up in front of him. Without even thinking anything about it, Cole clicked the X in the terminal window to force it to shut down.

Seconds later another black terminal window appeared on the screen.

"What the fuck?"

Words appeared on the terminal screen.

Genetics is an affront to God's creation.

Cole clicked the X to shut the window down. And again, it went away, for just a second. Then the terminal window appeared again. This time it took over the entire screen, blacking out the monitor's view.

The words appeared again.

Genetics is an affront to God's creation.

Cole pushed his chair back slightly from the workstation. "I.T. guy, whatever you name is, come look at this."

The I.T. guy meandered over, huffing slightly as if annoyed. "S'up?"

Cole pointed at the screen. "What is that? And why is it on my screen?"

"Uhhh, well, that's a new one for me." The I.T. guy motioned to Cole to leave the workstation. "I'm not sure what that is... did you click on something?"

Cole retorted, "No, I was just doing work."

Before the I.T. guy could respond, the screen blinked black and then came back.

Worry not, for I shall lay bare your transgressions.
The truth of your deeds will be shared with all.

The IT guy tapped at the screen. "I have no idea what that is or what that means but... what the..."

The screen went blank. The terminal appeared again, but everything else on the screen was gone.

"I don't know what you did but now we're stuck." Cole tossed his hands in the air and kicked the desk.

On the screen, the typing appeared again.

Behold.

"Oh shit." The I.T. guy jumped up from the chair. "I don't know what that program is or who is typing that, but my network monitor just blew up. We're somehow streaming data from this machine outbound. Streaming to Instagram and Facebook and..."

"What the fuck does that mean? Can I get back to my work and do my research or is this machine fucked?" Cole stomped his foot like an angry toddler.

"Dude, this machine is somehow now connected to the global

Internet. Your research is being posted online. On public forums, all the social media sites. Anyone, everyone can see this stuff." The I.T. guy stumbled backwards.

"That can't happen. My research is on the genetic makeup of some very nasty stuff. Literally. I have research in there that discusses the gene sequencing of some of the nastiest viruses on the planet. It's Pandoras box! And it's on fucking Twitter?" Cole screamed. "Stop it!"

The I.T. guy looked at Cole, his face pale. "Too late. It's already out."

The screen went black.

ACKNOWLEDGMENTS

Writing a nonfiction book is hard, writing a novel is harder. At least I think so. Doing research and putting that information into a digestible form for others to read is not new to me but using my feeble imagination to try and convey scenes and characters to the reader with an interesting narrative has been extremely difficult, but also very rewarding. This book, nor any of my personal successes, would have been possible without the experience I gained while serving in the US Navy as a Cryptologist. In that role I was exposed to the best and brightest our country had to offer and my time in that space literally decided my future. I am forever grateful and humbled to those that are serving and have served. I pray daily for those that have paid the ultimate price as part of their service to our great nation and I hope that in some small way my book helps others to become aware of the work and efforts of those warriors that serve in silence in windowless rooms, doing work that few can and less know is needed.

I'm eternally grateful to the multitude of women that I have had the good fortune to meet and learn from in my life. I have had the blessing to be influenced by heroes of mine like my mother, who never once said "no" to any challenge, my grandmother who built and ran a company for 4 decades in a male dominated field. My wife, who bravely stares death in the face as she serves her patients, and who selflessly took on my girls as her own daughters. To me these role models exemplify what I aspire to be and to emulate.

I am indebted to the talented, and smart women at Forrester Research who are literally changing and influencing the cyber security market report by report. Their work and dedication to helping others understand the intricacies of this market are critical to it's future and thanks to leaders like Laura Koetzle and Stephanie Balouras they have the power to collectively change our future.

A very special thanks to Wendy Nather for showing me what it means to personify grit and dedication to the job. To Heidi Shey for helping me understand the value that a career change might offer, and to the multitude of women in technology like them that have survived and thrived in this market despite the barriers that have been put in front of them.

To my editor Kristy, thank you for making my book suck less. And to my publishing lead, Juliet thank you for your kind consideration and focus on getting this book out quickly, efficiently, and with quality.

To my daughters. I hope someday you read this and see the power and prowess that women in this space (or any space for that matter) have, and I hope you too are inspired like I have been to do more than you think you can, and like all those that have blazed trails before you, to never give up and never think you "cant".

Finally, to anyone from anywhere, with any background that reads this book and is interested in this sector of technology.

Get your ass in gear, we need you!

9 781513 689876